I Will Call It Georgie's Blues

Also by Suzanne Newton

I Will Call It Georgie's Blues

A NOVEL BY

SUZANNE NEWTON

Puffin Books

PUFFIN BOOKS
Published by the Penguin Group
Penguin Books USA Inc.,
375 Hudson Street, New York, New York 10014, U.S.A.
Penguin Books Ltd, 27 Wrights Lane,
London W8 5TZ, England
Penguin Books Australia Ltd, Ringwood,
Victoria, Australia
Penguin Books Canada Ltd, 10 Alcorn Avenue, Toronto,
Ontario, Canada M4V 3B2
Penguin Books (N.Z.) Ltd, 182–190 Wairau Road, Auckland 10,
New Zealand

Penguin Books Ltd, Registered Offices: Harmondsworth,
Middlesex, England

First published in the United States of America by The Viking Press, 1983
Published in Puffin Books 1990
10 9 8

LIBRARY OF CONGRESS CATALOGING IN PUBLICATION DATA
Newton, Suzanne.   I will call it Georgie's blues / Suzanne Newton.   p. cm.
Summary: Because the Baptist minister's children in a small North
Carolina town have difficulty conforming to the roles their father
wishes them to play for public consumption, fifteen-year-old Neal
feels he must hide his consuming interest in jazz music.
ISBN 0-14-034536-1
  [1. Clergy—Family relationships—Fiction. 2. Family problems—
Fiction. 3. Jazz music—Fiction.] I. Title.
PZ7.N4875Iac 1990   [Fic]—dc20   90-8292

Printed in the United States of America
Set in Electra

FOR DEBORAH BRODIE

I Will Call It Georgie's Blues

Billy L. #19

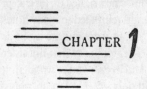

CHAPTER 1

Friday.

I put all the books in my locker except math and science and slammed it. There's something extra-satisfying about slamming a locker when the hall's empty and it echoes up and down. I hoped teachers were wincing in every room. I'd waited on purpose until the first wave left so I could walk home alone. All last period I'd been hearing the first few bars of Charlie Parker's "Cool Blues" in my head, and I was thinking what I could do with it on the piano.

"Hey, Neal!"

Pete Cauthin waved at me from the far end of the hall, then broke into a long-legged run that put him beside me in about five seconds. "Where you headed?'

"Home," I said.

Pete shook his head as he fell into step. His brown hair was frowsy from the humidity, and his pimples seemed more prominent than usual. "You'd never catch me doin' that. Go home and your mama finds somethin' for you to do. You never get away."

"Why are you still here?" I asked. "School was out a whole fifteen minutes ago."

He didn't pick up on the sarcasm. "I been coolin' my ass in Thompson's office for the better part of the day. He just let me go."

I didn't want to walk with Pete Cauthin. At age nineteen he

is already the Ultimate Bum. Unlike others of his type, he didn't drop out of school at age sixteen, although I'm pretty sure most of the high school faculty wishes he had. From what I've heard, he has systematically flunked every course he's signed up for except Industrial Arts. He's been suspended and reinstated so many times that everyone's lost count. In case you're wondering why he is talking to me, a lowly ninth grader, I regret to say that my sister Aileen claims him as her boyfriend. And in case you're wondering why I'm being so polite to him, I will only say that I'm not going to mix it with any guy whose muscles have a four-year advantage over mine. So I make it a point not to do anything to make Pete angry.

"Don'tcha want to know what I was there for?" he asked.

I stifled a sigh. Pete's such a regular in Thompson's office it's more newsworthy when he *isn't* there. "Sure."

"I made Miss Berkley cry," he said, laughing. "I don't know why she got upset just because I kissed her in front of the class. She ought to be flattered."

"Maybe you made her face greasy," I said. Right away I realized that wasn't very smart of me. His face turned slowly pink. I entertained notions of making a break for it, but for some reason Pete elected not to beat me up. Instead he turned on his heel and started walking away, but then he stopped and came back.

"I wasn't the only one in Thompson's office today. Aileen was there too."

"So?"

"So your dad won't like it much when he finds out."

"What kind of trouble is she in?"

"Let *her* tell you," he said, satisfied that he'd gotten my attention at last. "But I didn't have a thing to do with it. She'll tell you that."

"Well," I said, "it's her business."

He shrugged. "Your dad'll give her hell most likely. I mean, it don't look too good for the preacher's kid to be called to the office."

"Preacher's kids aren't any different from anybody else," I said stiffly.

"Maybe not, but they're supposed to be." His grin taunted me. I would gladly have stuffed my books down his throat, but getting into a fight with Peter Cauthin is about as productive as growing weeds. I stayed cool.

"I'll see you later," I said. "I've got to go by Bailey's store—I just remembered."

I turned right, and he didn't follow me, which was a good thing. I don't think I've ever come so close to punching him.

If Aileen intended to incite Dad's wrath, she showed real finesse in picking Pete for a boyfriend. I don't know what she sees in him, other than the fact that he's a true rebel, which is what she'd like to be. Dad won't let him come near our house, and Aileen is officially forbidden to go out with him. But she finds ways. Mom and Dad are counting on her going away to college next year as a way to get rid of him. Aileen doesn't want to get rid of him, which is probably a good thing for a lot of innocent people. If anyone else—boys, that is—gets friendly with her, Pete threatens to beat them up. The competition has all but disappeared.

I didn't have any reason to go to Bailey's store except to avoid walking with Pete, and now that I'd gone fifty feet out of my way, I began casting about for an excuse to turn around and go home. A guy doesn't just turn around in the middle of the sidewalk and start back in the direction he came from unless there's a reason. It looks stupid.

That's when I saw my little brother Georgie walking toward me. He didn't see me because he was looking at the ground in front of him. He's so skinny his head looks about a half size too large for him. The glasses don't help. Maybe the optometrist figured he'd grow into them, but he's been wearing them a year now, since he was six, and I can't tell that they fit any better than they did. In fact, he may have shrunk some.

I didn't really want to walk with him either—he asks so many serious questions it wears me out. But given a choice between him and Pete, I'll take Georgie any day.

It was as though my thoughts had traveled along a straight line and gotten him right between the eyes. He looked up and saw me. The sun flashed on the lenses of his glasses as he raised his arm and waved. I stopped and waited for him.

"You're coming from the wrong direction," I said as he caught up with me. I pointed east. "School's that way."

"I went down to Bailey's," he said vaguely. I saw that he was carrying a large folded-over paper sack on top of his schoolbooks.

"What for? Did you come into some money suddenly or something?"

He looked up at me quickly, studying my face. "No. I needed some things."

"That's a pretty good-size sack. How can you buy that much stuff on your allowance?"

"I made a deal with Mr. Bailey," he said in that funny grown-up way of his. "I'll be paying him my allowance for a while."

I stopped in my tracks. "You what? You mean he gave you credit?"

He nodded. "But I wish you wouldn't say anything about it to Mom or Dad. This is between Mr. Bailey and me."

I shrugged, and we walked on. I could understand his concern—Georgie and Dad don't get along too well.

"Neal, who is your favorite person in our family?" The question came out of his mouth in the matter-of-fact tone of a social scientist taking a poll or something.

"Oh, you, of course!" I laughed.

"I'm serious!" he said sternly.

"Well, gosh, I don't know! How can you have a favorite person in a family? Sometimes I like everybody. Sometimes I wouldn't give a nickel for any of you. That's not a fair question—somebody's bound to get their feelings hurt."

"Do you think Mom and Dad love me?" he asked.

The question struck terror in my heart, unexpected as it was. I've never been good at out-and-out lying, especially not to Georgie, who can read the back of my brain through my eyes.

"Who knows?" I blustered, scrambling for an answer that would be as true as I could make it. "I don't know if they love *me* or Aileen. I don't know what that means. Parents are supposed to love their children—it's a built in, like a bookcase or the plumbing. It comes with the package."

We had gotten to the corner of Salton and Water streets in front of the Gideon Baptist Church, where my father has been minister these fifteen years. I was born here, as a matter of fact. The bulletin board out in front said "Richard E. Sloan, Minister. 'Blessed Are the Peacemakers.'" Dad is not one to spend hours fretting over a catchy sermon title.

"I don't know how they *feel* toward you or me or Aileen. They're there and they do things for us and they let us live in the house. I take that as a pretty good sign."

My tone was light, and I kept watching his face the whole time I talked to see how he was taking it. He was going to do something with my answer, I was sure.

"I don't think they do," he said when I finally wound down, as though nothing I'd said made any difference. He was answering his own question.

"Well, I don't know how to persuade you, then," I said. "I think you're wrong. You just can't expect much from them in terms of lovey-dovey words and such."

"It's all right," he said. "It doesn't bother me all that much now."

I couldn't believe the conversation we were having. How many other guys have to put up with this kind of junk from their second-grade brothers? I changed the subject.

"What's in the sack?"

He hugged it and the books closer to him, as though he were afraid I might grab it and look in. "Just some stuff I needed."

"For what?"

Sometimes I think he has twice as many muscles in his face as other people, and they all seem out of control, especially when he's getting ready to make some outlandish statement. He has taken to doing that a lot lately. Dad calls it lying.

"No exaggerations now, Georgie," I said. "I'd rather not know anything than to have you tell me something that's not so."

He looked relieved. "What I need it for is a secret. Sometime I might tell you."

"Suits me," I told him. I am a great believer in privacy. Some things are nobody else's business.

We were almost home. I was perspiring in the April sunshine. Spring weather in North Carolina is tricky—you freeze in the mornings and burn up in the afternoons. My mind raced ahead to the freedom of a Friday afternoon—home for a quick snack, then maybe out to the ball field.

"Would you do me a favor?" Georgie interrupted my thoughts.

"Maybe. What?"

"Maybe you could go in first and talk to Mom or something until I can get to my room and put this stuff away."

He is a pretty cagey little person. Usually Mom is on his back as soon as he walks in. It's "Tell me what you did at school," or "Sit down and do your homework right now," or "Why did you do what I specifically told you not to?" Georgie is infinitely patient with her, but the more patient he is the more irritated she gets. I could see his reasoning. If I went in first and distracted her, he'd at least have a few private minutes in his room.

"Yeah, I'll do that." I grinned at him to make up for not being able to assure him that Mom and Dad loved him. He smiled back.

I made a lot of noise coming up on the porch, banging the screen door, going all the way back to the kitchen where I knew Mom would be. I got to the kitchen door as she was starting out.

"Hey, how about some cookies!" I roared. My voice has a satisfying depth it didn't have a year ago. Mom frowned.

"Don't be so loud, Neal! I'm not deaf."

I knew I was being obnoxious—I couldn't blame her for looking so put out. Behind me I heard the slight squeak of the front screen. Georgie sneaking in.

"Hey, hey, hey! Fat Albert here wants some cookies!" I bellowed, to cover up the sound. I blocked Mom's way, teasing. I'm taller than she is now, and sometimes I pretend that I'm going to break her in two or something because she's such a shrimp. But you have to watch it with her—she doesn't tease too well.

"Neal, what's the matter with you? I don't have time for this kind of foolishness!"

I counted to five slowly and then stepped aside. Georgie would be in his room by now. She pushed by me and went to the front door. After a minute she came back.

"I can't understand why Georgie's not home yet," she said. "Did you see him?"

"Oh, he probably stopped to look at something on the way," I said. "You know how he is." I went over to the cabinet and pulled down a box of vanilla wafers.

"Watch it now—those cookies have to last the rest of the week."

She says that every day. I hardly hear it any more.

"Mom—" I opened my mouth to say, "Georgie thinks you and Dad don't love him." But somehow the words got stuck just back of my teeth and wouldn't be said.

"What?"

"Nothing, I just remembered," I lied. I took my allotted stack of cookies, poured myself a glass of milk, and sat down at the table, watching her move around the kitchen.

Mom is a quick, sharp woman. Her hair is still as brown as mine, and she wears it back in a kind of ponytail. I think she's worn it that way ever since she was in high school, judging from her old yearbook pictures. She doesn't enjoy her life very much, I guess—at least her mouth is set in a straight line most of the time. It seems to me that when I was a little guy, Georgie's age, she smiled more and was softer. But maybe when you're little you don't notice things as much as when you get older.

"Have you done your homework?" she asked.

"Most of it. What's left I can do in thirty minutes."

"You always say that. Why do you have so little work to do at home?"

"I do it at school. Other people goof off—I use my time. Why not do it there and get it over with?"

She sighed. "I wish you were in a school that challenged you. If you had some competition, you'd find out you aren't the Albert Einstein you think you are."

She plopped floured chicken into hot grease, and the sizzle was loud and smoky. "You never have to do papers or projects. You're going to find out when you get to college."

I didn't say anything. She talks like it's my fault that the school isn't making me work harder. Can't you just see me going up to Mrs. Ricks and saying, "Mrs. Ricks, I just don't have enough to keep me busy. Couldn't you give me a little extra work to challenge my brilliant brain?" If the word got out, nobody'd ever speak to me again. I've got it set—I make B minuses. I know exactly when to put on the steam and when to let up. Nobody ever hears me begging for an extra point or letter grade—I could get them if I wanted to. Besides, I don't need to worry about such things in the ninth grade.

"If only we lived in a place that had a decent school." She seemed to be talking to herself more than to me, and again it was a refrain I've heard dozens of times. I used to take it seriously. When she talked about it, I thought maybe she intended to push Dad to get us out of Gideon, but nothing has happened. I want to leave. Nothing would please me more than to live in a place where the school was big enough to have a decent band and where I'd get to go to some concerts once in a while. And where more than one person in the whole town knew something about jazz.

"May I have some cookies?"

Georgie's clear voice came from the doorway. Mom spun around. "Oh, Georgie! You startled me. When did you come in?"

"Just a little while ago." He came into the kitchen. He has taken to appearing suddenly, almost from nowhere. You never hear him coming, and then you look up and he's standing beside you, and you have no idea how long he's been there. It's kind of spooky.

"You may have four," Mom said, getting them for him. She poured him a glass of milk, and he slid into the chair beside me. I watched her looking at him. Georgie's question had put a new light on things, and I tried to read her face. I realized, though, that I wasn't sure what to look for. How does a person look at you when they love you? Also, when you're around someone a lot, maybe habit keeps you from showing how you feel.

"What's the matter, Neal—has my face turned blue or something?"

I guess I was looking harder than I meant to. I shook my head. She turned her attention to Georgie, who was eating his cookies methodically, the way he does everything.

"Don't go out until you do your homework," she said.

"All right."

"And bring me the work, so I can see that you did it."

"Yes'm."

Since he didn't give her any resistance, there was nothing else for her to say. She went back to turning the chicken. I winked at Georgie. He winked back, but it's hard for him to close just one eye. His whole face screwed up in the attempt.

"I'll be at the ball field," I said, getting up to rinse my glass. "What time is dinner?"

"Six. Don't be late."

I thought, as I went out, how boring her life must be, saying the same things over and over again to the same people.

CHAPTER 2

"Bow your heads," Dad mumbled, already squinting and leaning toward his plate. I have learned to go down slowly, so as to take in what everyone else is doing during the blessing. Aileen's head doesn't bow, but she closes her eyes. I think she must count while he prays. Mom leans her head on one hand, like she's grateful for those few seconds to rest. Georgie—well, he is undergoing evolution. When he was really little, he would squeeze his eyes shut, clasp his hands together so tightly that the knuckles turned white, and bow his head so low that his hair touched the plate. I believe he thought it would please Dad. Now he doesn't put that much energy into it. Instead he flashes a funny look in Dad's direction before he closes his eyes.

"Bless, O Lord, these gifts to our use and our lives to Thy service, in Christ's name, amen." The words were proper but empty. The only time we get a variation is when company comes, which isn't often, and then Dad delivers a long, fancy blessing— the kind that outsiders expect from a Baptist minister.

As far as I'm concerned, it's just something we do so we can get on with the next thing, which is eating. Mom began passing the chicken. Aileen took a helping of beans, Dad's fingers drummed on the tablecloth while he waited for the stuff to get around to him

"What I want to know," said Georgie, sitting straight with his hands still in his lap, "is what does it mean?"

Irritation clouded Dad's face. "What does *what* mean, George?"

"The words you say. It doesn't make sense to me."

Most kids have little piping voices or soft fuzzy ones. Georgie sounds as though he got a set of vocal cords that were intended for a grown person. When he says something he commands attention, even when he doesn't mean to.

"In 'Bless these gifts to our use,'" Dad repeated, "we're asking God to help us use responsibly what He gives us. In 'Bless our lives to Thy service' we're asking God to help us serve Him in the way we live." He sounded like he was instructing a class instead of talking to a member of his own family.

"I think that we shouldn't bother God with it," said Georgie. "God can't make us behave. It sounds like asking God to make us behave."

Well, I'll be damned, I thought.

"Georgie, why do you always have to complicate things?" Aileen sighed. Her green eyes taunted Dad. "You'll make Dad so self-conscious about what he's saying he won't be able to use that blessing any more—he might have to get a new one."

My stomach muscles tightened. Georgie hadn't meant to start something, but he had.

"Well," said Mom unexpectedly, "I think Georgie has a point. I've wondered about that myself from time to time. Have a drumstick, Georgie."

He took his hands out of his lap and helped himself to the food. The knot in my belly loosened. I was relieved that Mom had come to the rescue—often no one does and things tend to go from bad to worse. Usually there isn't anyone to save the day, because nobody gets the best of Dad.

He is fifty-six, fifteen years older than Mom. Maybe that's why it's hard for him to look at things from our point of view—I guess he can't remember when he was eighteen or fifteen or seven. He definitely gives the message that he's pretty sold on his own opinions and that nobody can tell him anything. In the confines of our house he wears a perpetual scowl, because it seems like 've seldom do anything to meet his approval. On Sundays—or when anyone outside the family is looking—he puts on a plastic smile that's ten times worse. What I don't understand is that none of those outside the family seem to know it's plastic.

Dinner at home is not my favorite time of day. I can compare it to a game of dodge ball, where someone takes aim and tries to get you out, and you spend all your energy staying alert to keep from getting hit.

When I was younger I read in a magazine: "In order to make mealtimes pleasant one should discuss topics that are conflict-free." I spent days trying to think up topics that were conflict-free, but finally gave up. Everything—even sunflowers and white mice—leads to tears and shouting, or else silence, which is worse. I have concluded that the conflict is there, like it or not, and it will ride on any words that are spoken. So my contribution to family tranquillity is to keep my mouth shut.

"Aileen, what night is your graduation?" Mom asked. "You haven't put it on the kitchen calendar."

"I'm not sure about the date," Aileen said vaguely. "I'll have to check."

"You should send Gran an invitation. You're her oldest grand-child, after all. She'll want to come down."

Aileen didn't say anything. She's not too fond of Gran Rodgers in the first place. Gran is Mom multiplied in the do's and don'ts department.

"Aren't you supposed to pay cap and gown rental, too?"

Aileen's eyes flickered up to meet Mom's. Her auburn hair hung smoothly beside her face. I wondered for the umpteenth time how anyone so good-looking could be a member of our family.

"I suppose," she said.

"You'll have to let me know how much so I can write a check," Mom went on. "I may go ahead and call Gran before you mail the invitation, so she can plan ahead. You know how busy she is."

A typical Aileen remark would include a snide comment about

gallivanting grandmas and some cynical observations about primitive rituals. However, nothing like that was forthcoming.

"I hope you have your eye on a job for the summer," Dad said. "College expenses next year are going to be high. If you had the kind of academic record you ought to have, you'd have a scholarship."

Aileen gave him a withering look. "It was your big idea that I apply at Garber, not mine. It's so Baptist and full of women. Other places wouldn't cost so much."

Dad made an impatient gesture. His gray hair is thin and has a tendency to fly about because he lets it grow too long. It tends to make him look even more impatient than he is, if that's possible.

"We're not talking about the school," he said. "The issue is your lack of academic responsibility."

"Yes," she said, "and with all my advantages here at home there's no excuse for it, right?"

My stomach knotted again. Aileen should be gone from here for everyone's good, especially her own. She and Dad are always at war over something. Sometimes he starts it, sometimes she does. Times like this I get so furious I'm tempted to stand up, grab the edge of the tablecloth, and yank as hard as I can. I would yell like Tarzan. I think whatever happened afterward would be a small price to pay for that moment of satisfaction.

Aileen stood up suddenly, putting her napkin beside the plate. "May I please be excused? I feel sick."

And she did look sick. Her face was almost green, it was so pale.

"Yes, of course," Mom said, pushing away from the table as though she intended to follow, but Aileen rushed out and ran upstairs so quickly that Mom didn't have a chance.

"Let her alone," Dad muttered. "This way we don't have to watch her sulk."

"I think she's really ill," Mom said sharply.

"Hmph—she's just getting the worst of the argument, that's all."

It's a good thing he wasn't looking right at Mom that instant as I was. I could almost see a streak of fire flash from her eyes. Maybe she feels like jerking the tablecloth, too.

All this time Georgie and I had been eating, staying out of the line of fire, so to speak. But with Aileen gone the picture shifted. As in dodge ball, it's the people who're left who draw the attention of the ball throwers.

"Georgie, do you think you could possibly manage to eat without putting both elbows on the table?"

"Yes, sir." Georgie quickly removed his elbows.

"And you might try keeping your mouth closed when you chew."

Georgie sighed. It wasn't a loud sigh. I was sitting next to him and I barely heard it, but Dad was waiting for it.

"Young man, I'm trying to teach you manners so that when you're eating in someone else's company you won't disgrace us!"

"Yes, sir."

There wasn't a trace of ugliness in his response. I think that made Dad angrier than ever, because he likes resistance. He seems to think that proves he's right. Georgie drives him crazy just being here. He was old enough to be a grandfather when Georgie was born, and what little patience he had with kids was already worn threadbare. Mr. and Mrs. Watkins next door are always talking about how much their late-in-life daughter has meant to them, but I never hear that kind of talk from Dad about Georgie.

The telephone rang.

"It never fails!" Mom was exasperated. "I wish people would remember we have dinner at this hour and—"

"Now, Lou, you know very well that if someone needs me, I have to be available."

Mom went to answer the phone. Don't ask me why *he* doesn't answer it, since it's usually for him anyhow. If someone calls one of us during dinner—Aileen or Georgie or me—he won't allow us to talk to them.

She was gone a long time. We had just about finished eating

when she finally returned. She had a funny, stunned look on her face, as though what she'd heard hadn't sunk in yet.

"What is it, Lou?"

She shook her head and sat down. "I'll discuss it with you later, Richard." The food on her plate was cold, but she ate it anyway, chewing and chewing like some kind of machine.

Obviously Georgie and I weren't supposed to hear whatever it was. We took the hint and excused ourselves. I went up to do homework, and he went to his room, probably to look over the secret items he'd bought at Bailey's. Aileen's door was shut. I debated sticking my head in to see how she was feeling, but decided she'd think I was being nosy.

I got out the books I'd brought home and stacked them on the desk, but studying math and science was not what I wanted to do. With the door ajar I could hear my parents talking in the room below, but I couldn't make out the words. No sound at all came from Aileen's room, which bothered me more than I cared to admit.

My earliest memories of Aileen are of someone taller than me pushing me here, pulling me there, getting me to dress up in weird clothes, making me try things that would get me in trouble or hurt. I don't remember disliking her especially, just being wary a lot of the time.

I suppose we've done the usual fighting and scrapping, but mostly we stay out of each other's way. I have my room, she has hers. I go my way, she goes hers. I do not enter into the arguments that she and Dad have because—well, because I would not be welcomed by either side. Why waste the energy?

She was eleven when Georgie was born. She wanted him to be a girl, and when he turned out to be another boy she was vocal about her disappointment. She thought he was an ugly little creature—but she wasn't the only one who thought that. He really did look like a squirrel baby or something at first. He was sickly for a long time—a couple of times he nearly died. Anyway, she began looking after him, giving him his bottle, or rocking him to sleep and singing to him. She got attached to him in spite of herself, but she couldn't push and pull him the way she had done to me because he was too fragile. For about two years, until she and boys discovered each other, she was more his mother than Mom was. And then one day she turned into a beauty queen and left him behind in a cloud of dust.

I don't think he ever got over the suddenness of it. For a while he would follow her around at a safe distance, just in case she changed her mind, but she never did. He finally gave up. Since then I've taken more time with him, to sort of make up for it, but it isn't easy. He doesn't go for sports or any kind of rough-housing, and he doesn't play with other kids very much. He's not a sissy exactly—just frail.

The voices downstairs got louder. My mind drifted. I thought how Mrs. Talbot's piano could drown out all loud and unpleasant voices. I opened the desk drawer and took out some music manuscript paper, intending to write down the notes to "Cool Blues" that had been running through my head all day. But before I'd finished four bars I heard Mom's footsteps on the stair, quick and determined. Thinking she was after me for something I'd done— or not done—I stuffed the music back into the drawer and flipped my math book open.

But she passed my door and knocked on Aileen's. I heard Aileen say something, and then Mom went in. She didn't close Aileen's door, so I could hear, even if I hadn't been trying.

"I've had a call from Mr. Hampton," Mom began. "He says—"

"—that I'm flunking English and that I'm not going to graduate. I know."

There was a small silence, then Mom's exasperation. "Aileen, what are we going to do with you! If you were a slow learner or something it would be one thing, but you have a perfectly good mind. There's no excuse for it!"

"I'm not looking for excuses."

"What is your future going to be like? Are you going to do like Pete Cauthin and spend the rest of your days in Gideon High

School, trying to pass one course or another?"

"You couldn't stand that, could you? All you care about is that you've got to explain why your bright daughter didn't manage to graduate with others her age. How embarrassing for you!"

I don't see how Aileen has the nerve to talk to Mom like that. In the silence that followed, I filled in things I would say to Aileen if she were *my* kid.

"Would you kindly tell me," Mom said at last in measured tones, "what you think we—your dad and I—should do?"

"Sure. I think you should leave me alone. I'm the one flunking English, not you. I don't know why Mr. Hampton called you in the first place. He ought to know there's nothing you can do about it."

"Aileen—" Mom sounded desperate, helpless, angry. I could imagine Aileen sprawled across the unmade bed, not looking at Mom, and Mom standing just inside the doorway, trapped probably in the only clear space on the floor, her arms folded tightly across her chest, fingers gripping her upper arms.

Then the quick steps again, down the hall and the stairs, and a door slamming below.

I took a deep breath—I think I'd forgotten to breathe while all that was going on—and went out into the hall.

"Hey, Aileen—may I come in?" I spoke through the small crack of her door.

"I guess."

I went in, and there she was just as I'd thought, sprawled on the bed. She picked at a loose thread in the blue comforter. Her face had no expression. Her red hair fell loosely, dripping alongside her cheeks and spreading out on either side.

'What do *you* want?"

I sat on the little ruffly seat in front of her dressing table.

"I overheard. I guess I came to find out what you have in mind."

She quit picking at the thread, turned over and sat up. "What I have in mind? About what?"

"Life."

She rolled her eyes and flopped backward. The bed bounced. "What's it to you, squirt?"

The name didn't even sting, since I'm about six inches taller than she is. "Well," I said, "this household is not the greatest place in the world. Personally, I'm planning to do whatever I have to to get away from it at the appointed time. You hate it worse than I do, so why are you so determined to fix things so you can't leave?"

She sat up again. "Who says I can't leave?"

"Far as I know, you're without funds. There aren't any decent jobs here to help you earn some. You can't go anywhere else because you don't have enough capital even to rent a room to live in. And now that you won't have a high school diploma, you can't even go away to college. The way I look at it, you're trapped. And you've done most of the trap-building yourself."

"My, aren't you the righteous one!"

That did sting. I almost got up and went out. "Look, Aileen, I don't want you to get stuck here. But you might have to do what's expected of you just to get away. I mean, you're cutting off your nose to spite your face."

She turned away with disgust. Her eyes were tired. I felt sorry that she didn't have someone like Mrs. Talbot to talk to, but she'd systematically made enemies of all the adults she knew.

"Just don't worry about me," she said, closing me out. "You have a plan for yourself that includes sucking up to everyone you have to. That's just dandy."

"Is there any way you can pass that English course?"

"No," she said flatly.

"How about summer school—could you take it again in summer school?"

"Look, would you please quit acting like you're my guardian?"

"O.K., O.K." I got up. "I just wondered if there was anything to be done—"

"No! Just get out!"

So I did.

I didn't go back to my room. Instead I went downstairs, walking lightly so Mom and Dad wouldn't hear, and went out.

CHAPTER 3

I stood on the front porch for a moment, where I could see a strip of the river between Mrs. Talbot's house and the Masons' garage. Sometimes I wish that our house was on that side of the street, so the river would be in our backyard, but I suppose this piece of property was cheaper. Our house was built in the mid-forties—two-story brick, pitched roof, littly boxy rooms. I prefer the one Mrs. T. lives in—contemporary design, cypress exterior that blends with the trees. When I go inside it, I feel that I'm outside because of the skylights and the large windows overlooking the river.

I ambled down the steps and across the street.

"Neal!"

Mom's voice, sharp at my back. I turned. "Yes, ma'am?"

"Come here a minute."

I retraced my steps. She stood half in, half out of the screen doorway.

"I don't think it's a good idea for you to be forever pestering Jeanette. Hardly a day goes by that you aren't over there. You shouldn't impose on her that way."

"Hey!" I said. "What brought that on? Has Mrs. T. complained to you or something?"

"No, she hasn't. I hope it doesn't come to that—that's the reason I'm telling you to think about it now, before she *has* to complain."

I could feel anger beginning way down in my stomach, but I tried to keep it light.

"Well, we're good enough friends—I think she'd tell me if it was getting to her. In fact, when I drop by, if she's busy she just tells me to come back later. It's no problem—"

"Neal, I know what I'm talking about. I don't want to forbid you to go over there, but you have to be more . . . more considerate."

How do you know what you're talking about? I wondered. Just because it annoys you for people to drop in unexpectedly, why should you think Mrs. T. feels that way? I didn't say it, though. I'm not dumb.

"All right," I said. "I'll go down to the landing."

I could feel her eyes on me as I walked down the street toward the boat landing. Maybe she thought that as soon as she went inside I'd go straight to Mrs. Talbot's.

Maybe I would.

Mrs. T. and I have been friends for two years. She came to Gideon out of nowhere—created quite a sensation since nobody new comes here much. She wasn't kin to anyone in town, and she didn't have any business connections. She rented a house on the edge of town and bought the vacant lot on the river next to the Masons'. The builders came almost immediately.

Frankly, I wasn't too happy about that, because until then we had an unrestricted view of the river from our front porch. The prospect of looking into someone's window instead wasn't so wonderful. I remember making snide remarks at the time, mostly echoing what I'd heard the grown-ups say in the churchyard on Sunday. Meanwhile Mrs. Talbot began giving piano lessons in the little house she was renting while hers was being built.

One Sunday she came to Dad's church.

In these parts winter days are bone-chilling and windy. It seldom snows, but from December to March a person goes around permanently goose-pimpled. The sanctuary of Gideon Baptist

Church is especially depressing in winter, and not just because it's hard to heat. It is a frame structure that smells like the inside of an old lady's travel trunk. Looks like one, too. The carpet in the middle aisle is the dark maroon stuff that was popular eighty years ago. The floor under it buckles and turns—walking on it feels like stepping on live animals. The stained glass windows are mostly purple, which makes everyone look sort of sick. The piano sits on one side of the pulpit and an electric organ on the other. There's something discouraging about the place even in summer when the windows are open, but in winter it's pretty unbearable.

The day Mrs. T. walked in, wearing a red wool suit and with her blond hair twisted into some kind of dramatic-looking knot, the church seemed to warm right up. Mom, Aileen, Georgie, and I were in the pew across the aisle from her. Since I was closest to the end, I could turn my head from time to time and look without being too conspicuous. She was a refreshing sight, like a cheery hearth fire.

After the service lots of people came up to speak to her, some who already knew her because of the piano lessons. Before I could escape, Mom had me by the shoulder and was introducing me to Mrs. T. When Mrs. T. stuck out her hand and I shook it, I was surprised at the strength of her grip.

"Do you like music, Neal?" she asked.

"Yeah, I guess," I mumbled. "I don't know too much about it."

"Would you like to?"

I started to say no, but something happened between my brain and my mouth, and it came out, "I might."

She smiled and winked. "Come to see me, then."

The truth is, I didn't want to take piano lessons—guys in Gideon don't do things like that—but I was curious about Mrs. Talbot, so I made a point of going by her rented house a few days later and offering to do chores for her. She let me fill up the woodbox and carry out the garbage and fix a broken hinge on the back door. She didn't have a music student during that half hour, so the whole time I was there she sat at her grand piano and played sounds such as I'd never heard. That was my first introduction to jazz, and I fell in love. I wanted it for myself. She knew, but she made me ask for it.

"Look," I said, and even now I get embarrassed when I think about how I must have sounded, "I don't mind taking piano lessons, but I don't want anybody to know about it—not *any-body*."

Her eyebrows went up, two question marks. "Do you really think you can keep a secret in Gideon?"

"It may not be easy," I said, "but it's possible. *You* have secrets—" As soon as the words left my mouth, I wanted to bite off my own tongue. I didn't need a mirror to tell me how red my face was.

"I've had more practice," she said, unoffended. "I've lived in places where secrets are allowed. It's not a matter of hiding so much as it is keeping one's business to one's self."

"I can do that," I said. "I'll have to work out my lessons by doing things for you. I don't want my folks to know."

"What do you think they would do if they knew?"

I shrugged. "It just wouldn't belong to me any more. They'd nag me to play in front of people. After a while I wouldn't know whether I was doing it because I wanted to or because they wanted me to."

I wasn't sure I was making myself clear, but she nodded. "All right, we'll try it for a while. We may renegotiate later. One thing you have to consider—you'll have to practice. How do you plan to do that without anyone finding out?"

It was true I hadn't even thought of that part. "I'll figure it out," I said. I remember walking home in a daze that afternoon, not feeling the chill. Someday I'd be able to make the piano sound that way. My hands fairly itched.

They still do, only now it's worse. They long to be on a keyboard all the time. No one in Gideon knows I study piano with Mrs. T., even though they see me hanging around her house. So far as they know, I'm just the chore boy.

I've learned a lot from her, not just about music but about other places and people. I've never heard a live performance, but Mrs. T. has heard all the greats. She has every recording that's worth owning, and books about jazz from the twenties until now. I've read everything I could and listened to the records for hours. But the best part is hearing her tell about the times she heard Erroll Garner, Theo Monk, Charlie Parker, Dizzy Gillespie, and so many others whose names are legendary.

She must've been a free-wheeling person when she was young, hanging around nightclubs and all. She studied music in college, but she loved jazz and she sneaked around to hear it. Sometimes she'd stay out all night and leave a pillow dummy in her dormitory bed.

"Wasn't it kind of hard?" I asked. "Not sleeping, and then having to go to classes and all?"

"Yes, it was—but I had to do it to get what I wanted."

"And you never got caught?"

She smiled. "Yes, once. The dean read me the riot act—didn't I know how terrible it was for a respectable young lady to be seen in those dark, smoky places with drug addicts and prostitutes and other bad characters? What would people think?"

"Yeah—that's what Dad would say," I said.

She laughed outright. "The poor woman had never been in a nightclub in her life. She was convinced that anything carried on under the cover of darkness was of the devil—including jazz."

"What happened?" I asked.

"After I finished school I went to Chicago."

"But why are you here in Gideon?" I had no business asking, but it burst out of me because I couldn't understand. If she loved music so much, why had she come to this nothing place where jazz was more foreign than Greek?

Sadness moved over her face and then was gone, as if a hard

pain took her and then let go. She shook her head. All she said was, "Maybe I came here to discover you."

I wouldn't bring it up again, mostly because I don't like for her to be sad. But I've wondered what she left behind when she came here. Where's Mr. Talbot? Did she ever have any kids? Why did she pick Gideon, of all places? Someday she might tell me, but it's up to her. They are her secrets.

I don't know whether she's tired of keeping mine, but she won't tell until I give the word. Meantime, I've worked out ways and means. When I'm pretty sure no one will come in, I sneak into the church to practice my licks and improvise, figure out wild chord combinations and rhythms, pretend I'm Erroll Garner or Bud Powell playing for people who love this music. I feel like laughing—or crying—on Sunday mornings when Miss Lola Phifer falters through "Blessed Assurance" on the same keys. Mrs. T. makes me work hard on technique—she says there's no substitute for it and that my fingers will never do what I want them to unless I practice. During the school year I sometimes leave the house early in the morning under the pretext of doing some special project at school, but actually it's to practice on Mrs. T.'s piano before her teaching day begins. Usually on Saturdays I can count on a couple of uninterrupted hours there, but if Mom was serious about cracking down on my visits, I had a real problem.

At the landing a dozen or so people waited their turn to launch their boats. Winters they bring the boats up to scrape barnacles, caulk, and repaint, but in late spring when the weather gets warm for good, they bring them down here on trailers to slide them back into the water. I can almost hear the boats sigh when they slip back in after being out of their element for so many months. I feel that way when I can get to a piano.

I stood and watched for a while, but Mom's words weighed me down. I knew I had to talk to Mrs. T. tonight, before some curtain was drawn down between us that would make me too self-conscious to mention it.

My mind made up, I turned around. There was Georgie, not ten feet away.

He grinned. "I was going to sneak up on you."

"It's a good thing you didn't," I growled. "I'm in a bad mood."

He was instantly serious. "What's the matter?"

I made a face. It was too much trouble to explain, and I told him so. He seemed to understand and didn't ask any more questions. I appreciate that about him. He's strange, but he isn't a pest like some little kids. We walked in silence up the quiet evening street. Most folks were inside, still eating dinner or cleaning up after.

"I'm going over to Mrs. T.'s, Georgie," I said when we were in front of the house. "She has a book I need for a report I'm doing in English class." I started to ask him not to tell Mom, but thought better of it. No reason to make him lie for me—he has enough problems.

"O.K." He stopped where he was, as though I'd drawn a line he was forbidden to cross over. "I might sit on our steps and wait for you."

I tousled his hair. "All right, but if Mom calls you in, don't give her some story about promising me you wouldn't move from the spot until I came back, you hear?"

I went up the angled steps to the side deck and rang the bell. Usually I just walk in, or open the door and call, but Mom's words had done their damage. After a few seconds Mrs. T. opened the door. When she saw it was me, her eyes widened.

"For Heaven's sake, Neal—what is this, ringing the doorbell?" She stood aside for me to come in. "I couldn't imagine who was visiting at the sacred hour when All Gideon Eats!"

The feeling came over me that always does when I enter this house. I don't know how to explain it, except to say this-is-where-I-belong. But Mom said this *wasn't* where I belonged.

Mrs. T. was having dinner. She cut me a slab from a freshly baked loaf of bread and made me sit at the table in front of the window. She smiled, her eyes probing. "You have a funny look on your face. What has happened?"

"Well," I said, "there isn't a delicate way to bring this up, so I'll just level with you And I expect you to level with me."

She sat back in the chair. "O.K. Sounds serious."

I told her what Mom had said, as close to word for word as I could. "The more I think about it, the madder I get," I said when I'd finished.

"Why?"

"She doesn't understand how it is, because she's not like you. But the problem is, all of a sudden it makes me think that maybe I *have* been inconsiderate, taking for granted that I could walk in and out of here like it was my own house or something. I guess part of it is that I'm mad at myself for not thinking of it before she said anything."

It seemed to me my words were garbled. I looked at her helplessly. "So what I want to know is is Mom right?"

"Yes and no."

The answer was prompt and even, like she had been waiting for the day to arrive when we would be talking about this very thing.

"You should've told me," I said.

She shook her head. "No, I have some selfishness about it, too. I've been thinking about that." She got up and went into the kitchen. In a few minutes she returned with a glass of wine for herself and a Coke for me.

"The truth is, you've been like a son to me, and sons go in and out unbidden. It may be that in the last couple of years you've been more my son than your mother's. I've liked it. You and I have developed a pattern, a rhythm. We know what to expect of each other. We've learned each other's likes and dislikes. It has been a very comfortable arrangement. I haven't felt that my privacy was invaded. I've always known I could tell you when I needed to be alone."

"That's what I tried to tell Mom," I said eagerly. "She doesn't understand that—"

She held up a hand. "Neal, you are not my son. In a way we've been playacting. The reality is that you are her son and my piano student. And remember that no one knows that you're my piano student—they can't even think about you in that context, because you don't want it known."

The words fell heavily between us. I looked at the shiny surface of the maple table, and I had the same feeling as when I wake up from a good dream and it's a school morning and I'm in the same old place.

"Well, there's one thing you left out," I said gruffly. "We're friends, too."

She nodded and smiled a little. "Yes, I know. And again, that's part of the problem."

"I don't get it."

"Our friendship keeps you from trying to be friends with your own folks. That may be what your mother is feeling."

I flung myself out of the chair and went over to another window. The river's surface moved slowly away from the setting sun. I thought of a phrase of music that would sound like that movement looked, sun and river separating, going away from each other. Sun would come up tomorrow, though, at the other end of the river. Then the river would be flowing toward it. They'd be meeting again. . . .

"She's jealous."

"That's putting it harshly," Mrs. T. said. "It's hard on parents when their kids get to be teenagers and don't like them any more. Perhaps they feel betrayed, after all they've been through on their children's account."

"Look, Mrs. T., my folks have never been friends to me or Aileen or Georgie—maybe not even to each other! They don't care about what we think or what we want or what we hope! All they care is that we don't act in any way that will disgrace them in this town!"

The words burned in my throat and mouth like acid vomit. The shock of speaking them made tears come to my eyes.

Mrs. T. sat very still. She didn't try to comfort me or deny what I'd said. After a while I came back to the table and sat, taking a big swallow of Coke so the lump in my throat would go down and I could talk.

"Please don't ask me to give this up," I said, when I could.

"I'm not asking you, Neal," she said gently. "But both of us need to take a good look at it—to be honest. To find a form that's appropriate, just the way we do in music. I feel a responsibility to do that—even though I like the way things are—especially now that your mother is concerned."

I will only hate Mom for making this happen, I thought. It's no way to begin a friendship with her.

"It may be that this is the time when people have to know about your music," she went on. "It is an explanation—a context. Keeping such a tremendous secret takes a lot of energy. Hiding is the hardest thing a person can do. And it isn't just the fact that you're studying music that's hidden—it is who you are, the real Neal Sloan."

"I'll think about it," I muttered, but I knew I didn't have the slightest intention of changing my mind. "I guess I'd better go home. May I have that *Encyclopedia of Jazz* you said I could borrow to do my report?"

"Sure." She went to the bookcase. I watched her long fingers tracing titles until she found the right book. I took it from her, not wanting to look her in the eye because I was feeling mean and ashamed.

"Yes, think about it," she said. "We'll work something out."

I nodded and went out the door she held open for me. The latch clicked behind me as I stood on the deck, and it seemed to me to be an unnecessarily loud and final sound.

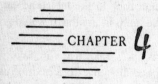

CHAPTER 4

Sunday was one of those perfect spring days when the morning is cool and warm at the same time, and the breeze carries a light scent of blossoms. It was never meant to be wasted in such a gloomy place as Gideon Baptist Church. I took deep gulps of air as I trailed several yards behind the others, thinking that maybe if I inhaled enough on the way to church the stifling atmosphere inside couldn't overwhelm me.

"Neal, quit dragging your feet. We're going to be late as it is!" Mom called over her shoulder. She was pushing Georgie forward with her hand between his shoulder blades. I know exactly what if feels like—she used to do that to me, too. Aileen was striding ahead as though she didn't want to be identified with any of us.

Being late to Sunday school is an ongoing ambition of mine. I hate sitting in the molded plastic chairs that line the walls of the Sunday school classroom. Mr. Lakeland, the teacher, is what Dad calls a "nice, sincere young man." His sincerity could almost make a person cry—he has absolutely no sense of humor. I think he was already old when he was born. I really miss Chuck Forrest, the guy who teaches junior highs. *He* remembers what it's like to be our age.

I could hardly move my shoulders in the confines of my suit coat. I've gotten too broad in the shoulders for it, but Mom says I have to wear it for another few months because there's no need to invest in a new suit while I'm growing so fast. She let out the pants legs as far as they'll go, but my socks still show, and the faded line where the pants used to be turned up is very obvious. It's dumb to have to dress like this anyhow. None of the other guys have to wear a suit—they can wear a decent pair of pants and a shirt without even a tie. I have to put on the whole outfit because I'm the preacher's son and it wouldn't look nice to dress casually for church.

"Neal."

"I'm coming, I'm coming!" I tried to make my voice sound faster, but my feet moved as slowly as possible. She finally just gave up and went on into the church without me, which suited me fine. This way I can delay going to Sunday school class until the last minute.

The main thing on my mind was Friday night's conversation with Mrs. T. She hadn't said that I absolutely couldn't visit any more without checking ahead of time, but it felt to me as though she were leaning that way. I had lain awake until midnight thinking about the difference it would make in my life. Maybe if I didn't bring it up again, things could still be the same between us.

But the fact is, I know that from now on Mom will make a point of asking me where I've been when I come in, just as she does Georgie. If I've been at Mrs. T.'s, I'll have to lie. That's why I didn't go over to practice yesterday as I usually do. It was a very long Saturday.

I turned and looked back down the street at Mrs. T.'s house nestled among the budding trees. It seemed to me that a wall, invisible but solid, had been thrown up around it, leaving me stranded outside.

"Hey, are you coming in or not?"

I looked around to see Aileen leaning out of the window of the Sunday school classroom.

"What's it to you?" I said, but not very loud.

She made a face at me and withdrew. I was close enough now to hear the babble of voices inside. Probably she wished she were out here with me. She has plenty on her mind, too. At breakfast yesterday Dad had pronounced judgment: because she was failing English and wouldn't graduate with her class, she was not to go out at night for any reason unless she was with a responsible adult. She couldn't use the car. She would have to come home immediately after school every day, and she had to spend at least three hours each day studying. He would personally check every assignment to see that it was complete.

I had watched her out of the corner of my eye. She was pale, but for once she didn't argue. All the time he spoke, she kept her eyes on her plate. When he was done she acknowledged what he said with a nod, but I had a feeling that she had plans of her own.

It seemed strange that all of a sudden she and I were in the same boat. It had been easy enough to tell her what she ought to do when I still had my haven, my hiding place. But now that it appeared I might lose it, I began to have some idea why a person like Aileen would be driven to desperate acts.

Mr. Lakeland was just getting up from his chair to close the door when I walked in. He isn't more than thirty-five, but his brown hair is already too thin to cover his scalp. Besides Dad, Georgie, and me, he's about the only other male here who wears a suit on a spring Sunday.

"Well, Neal—I thought maybe you'd been kidnapped!" That nervous, hearty laugh makes my ears ache. I looked away from him toward the others and crossed my eyes. There were a few satisfying snickers.

Because I was late, the choice of seats was limited. Usually all of us ninth graders sit in a clump on one side of the room, while all the juniors and seniors sit on the other side. Sophomore girls snuggle up to the older group, and sophomore boys tend to cast their lot with us—it makes them feel superior. There were two empty seats left—one beside Patty Briggs, the world's all-time homeliest ninth grader, and the other beside Aileen. Given a choice, no self-respecting guy would sit with his own sister. I went over and sat beside Patty. She looked as though she might quit breathing.

Mr. Lakeland cleared his throat. "All right, now," he began. "I think we can get started."

He didn't sound too sure about it, so the class didn't stop chattering. While he shuffled through papers on his lap, I took a quick look around the room.

Same crowd. Aileen in the far corner looking out the window. Beside her, two senior girls whispering to each other about something obviously unrelated to Sunday school—they were enjoying it too much. Assorted others, coming to a grand total of twenty. Patty Briggs squirmed and crossed one leg over the other nervously. I started to tell her not to do that, it would cut off her circulation, but caught myself just in time. She might think I was admiring her legs. I pressed my shoulder blades against the back of the plastic chair and prepared to put my brain in neutral for the next forty-five minutes.

"Our lesson today has to do with reconciliation," Mr. Lakeland announced. "Get out your Bibles."

We all looked at each other. Nobody but Betsy Brown had a Bible. Consternation showed in Mr. Lakeland's face. "You really *should* bring your Bibles," he fretted. "It's very difficult. . . ."

He sighed in the face of our stony uncooperativeness. "Well, then." He flopped open his little black King James and told us he was going to pass it around. Each of us was to look up and read aloud a verse, which he would assign. A snoring sound came from somewhere on the other side of the room, followed by a general discontented mumble. Mr. Lakeland ignored it and handed the Bible to Ham Parker at the beginning of the row of chairs.

Nobody can half read. It's boring to listen to, especially when they stumble over King James English with all its wherefores and haths. I tuned it out and closed my eyes. A fragment of music slid into my head, doing slow turns at first, but then picking up tempo and breaking into tricky rhythms that made their way into my fingers and feet. It was hard to keep still. This was something new. After church I'd jot down the ideas in my music notebook to help me remember until I could get to a piano to try it out. I went over it again, so I wouldn't lose it.

"Neal, will you read from the Gospel of Matthew, chapter five, verses twenty-three and twenty-four?"

I blinked and sat up, still thinking about the music. Patty handed me the floppy Bible and I fumbled through the thin pages for Matthew.

"Therefore if thou bring thy gift to the altar, and there rememberest that thy brother hath ought against thee; Leave there thy gift before the altar, and go thy way; first be reconciled to thy brother, and then come and offer thy gift."

I read the words aloud and slapped the book shut, handing it on to Jim Price, one of the tenth graders.

"Just a minute, Neal," Mr. Lakeland said. "Can you say that portion for us in everyday English?"

I couldn't even remember what I'd read—I hadn't been listening to myself. Why'd he have to keep picking on me? I reached for the Bible and found the passage again, not trying to hide my disgust.

"Well, I guess it says . . . er . . . if you're bringing your offering, and . . uh . . . you happen to remember that your brother is mad at you for some reason, you should leave the offering there and go apologize or whatever. Then come back and give the offering."

I slapped the Bible shut again. That was the last word I intended to say on the subject.

"Boy, *I* sure wouldn't do that!" Jim Price spoke up. "What if somebody came along and stole the offering while you were off apologizing? Shoot—I'd keep it right in my pocket!"

Mr. Lakeland gave him a look that was somewhere between disapproval and disbelief. "Jim, I rather doubt, if you'd been around in the days when this was written, that you'd carry the offering in your pocket. It was probably an animal."

Almost everybody in the class laughed, but not too much. We

didn't want Mr. Lakeland to look good at Jim's expense.

Aileen spoke from her place by the window. "I don't suppose that means just your regular blood brother, does it?"

Mr. Lakeland's eyes filled with hope. "Of course not! It means any person you have a relationship with or an obligation to—a friend, a neighbor." He was delighted that a question had come from the group, especially from the preacher's daughter. He usually tries to get us to talk by asking dumb questions that have only one answer. Anybody ought to know that there won't be any discussion if it's all cut and dried.

"But it *could* mean your brother . . . or sister . . . though, couldn't it?" Aileen persisted. "Or son or daughter?"

I looked at her hard, trying to figure her angle. There was a certain fierce mischief in her eyes that I have come to know well. Watch out, Mr. Lakeland!

He wiggled with excitement. Two whole questions in the space of a minute—what a challenge! "Absolutely! Now, what do you suppose happens if you give your offering when you haven't made peace with someone you've wronged?"

"Nothing," I said. I don't know why I let that slip out. It was a mistake.

He stiffened. "Would you like to explain further, Neal?"

"Not really," I mumbled.

"I think we'd all like to hear what you have to say."

"Well," I said, "people all over this congregation are on the outs with each other for one thing and another, and aren't *about* to apologize. But look at all the offering that goes into the plate every Sunday. Nothing happens. I mean, the money's collected and spent. What would you expect to happen—that it'll turn into toads or ashes or something? Or maybe that a bolt will come down out of the sky and burn it up?"

I glanced in Aileen's direction. Her eyes danced.

The silence lengthened while Mr. Lakeland gathered his forces. The eyes of the class were on him, curious as to how he and Jesus would work themselves out of this.

"I think you misunderstand, Neal, the significance of the passage." He was perspiring. His forehead gleamed softly. He glanced at his watch to see how much longer he had to be responsible. I was pretty sure he wouldn't call on me again for a long time.

"What *is* the significance, Mr. Lakeland?" Aileen asked sweetly.

"Well, it has to do with what happens to the persons, not the offering, you see." He began to read aloud from the "Teacher's Guide," clinging to it like a drowning man holds to a floating log. I think he hoped to find words of wisdom, but I certainly didn't hear any. The class lost interest and sat in a kind of stupor. I folded my arms and stretched out my legs as far as they would go, examining the scuffed toes of my shoes. The music came back into my head, brighter than ever.

It kept me going through the rest of the morning—Dad's sermon, Lola Phifer's playing, and all. By the time Dad pronounced the benediction and dismissed the congregation a little after twelve, I was burning to try on Mrs. T.'s piano the ideas that were beating around in my brain. I thought I had figured a way to do it, with Mom's blessing.

I crossed the churchyard to where Mrs. T. was talking with Mrs. Pendleton, a soft-looking gray-haired woman who attracts children the way sweets draw bees. She has taught the kindergarten class since before I was born. I remember her mainly for not fussing at us when we spilled our grape juice snack, and for complimenting my modeling clay snakes. Mrs. Pendleton gave me a big smile and patted my arm.

"Oh, you're getting so tall, Neal!" she exclaimed. "Isn't he, Jeanette? It seems like no time at all since he was running in and out among us after church, and now here he is standing about like a grown person!"

"I think it would cause problems if I tried running in and out now," I said. "Some people might get knocked down."

They both laughed. "Well, maybe," said Mrs. Pendleton, "but it's a shame, isn't it, to get so large and dignified that you can't play any more? Playing never hurt anyone so far as I know."

Mrs. T. nodded. "Yes—but not playing probably does."

I was interested in spite of myself. "What's the cutoff age? I mean, when can I expect to wake up one morning and not know how to play any more?"

"Oh, I hope never!" Mrs. Pendleton said fervently. "What you play may change year after year, but you must never forget how to have fun, because if you do, then—"

"—then you don't want anybody else to have fun either—right?" I finished, suddenly understanding. I tried to imagine Mr. Lakeland running, hopping, doing somersaults, playing cowboys or war, getting sweaty in a rough game of basketball. The idea was downright ridiculous.

"Well, I'm not sure of *that*," she said, casting about for words. "It's just that playing helps you remember what it's like to be a little person. For the sake of the little people, we grown-ups need to remember."

Mrs. T. looked at me and winked. "I agree, and for the sake of those who aren't so little, too."

"Well," I said, "maybe I have a few years left before decay sets in. I'll try not to get too dignified."

Mrs. Pendleton brightened. "Oh, it's not so hard. Look." She pointed to the edge of the churchyard where Chuck Forrest was horsing around with some of the junior highs. It made me kind of sad not to be included in the bunch.

"I have to be going now," I said. "Mrs. Talbot, I'd like to return the book I borrowed from you. What about sometime this afternoon, if it's convenient?" I couldn't believe I was talking to her this way—it was so formal, like acting in a play.

She gave me a quizzical look. "Sure—any time. I'll be home."

"All right. I'll see you later then. Good-bye, Mrs. Pendleton." I finished my part and walked away, feeling like a person made of pasteboard and wood. But at least the first piece of my plan was in place.

"I borrowed a book from Mrs. T. on Friday," I said to Mom

later as we walked home. "She said it would be convenient if J returned it this afternoon."

Mom got that tightness around her mouth that I hate so much. "Well, I suppose it's all right, so long as you don't spend the entire afternoon. I had hoped you might be around to keep an eye on Georgie. I'm getting one of my headaches, and I—"

"I won't stay long," I said, cutting her off. She's always getting those headaches. Sometimes I wonder if they're real.

"Maybe you could take Georgie with you," she said, "since you won't be staying long."

Cold rage flared in me so suddenly that I had to turn away to keep her from seeing. "Maybe I'll do that," I said, even and offhand. I wasn't going to say or do anything that would make her insist or force me to promise. I was glad Georgie had run on ahead of us, too far to hear her suggestion. I don't like breaking promises to him, even promises I don't make.

I thought the time would never pass. After lunch I went to my room to work on a paper and some algebra. What I actually did was to add to the pages in my notebook the stuff that had been going through my head all morning. I couldn't wait for Mrs. T. to see it. She'd be excited.

The house was super quiet—Mom was lying down nursing her headache, Dad was out visiting church members. Aileen was in her room, supposedly reading. The only person I couldn't really account for was Georgie. On impulse I decided to tell him where I was going, even though I didn't plan to take him with me.

I gathered my things, careful to place Mrs. T.'s copy of the *Encyclopedia of Jazz* on top of my notebook. Just as I opened my door, I saw the top of Aileen's head disappearing downstairs. Her feet made no sound on the carpeted steps. Shortly, the front door clicked open and a moment later closed again.

I took a deep breath and exhaled, surprised at the heavy thumping of my heart. Aileen was already breaking parole, and here I was, glad of it. At the same time I was scared for her. God, she had nerve! I'd spent an entire morning creating an elaborate plan of escape that wouldn't get anyone's disapproval, and Aileen was simply going out. Period. Why couldn't I be like that? I'm bigger than she is.

Still pondering my cowardice, I went over and tapped on Georgie's door. I waited a few seconds, then tried the knob. Suddenly the door opened inward, and Georgie gazed up at me, his face sightly flushed.

"Hi!" I said. "You were so quiet I thought you'd gone."

The light from the window reflected in his glasses, making his eyes unusually owlish. "No," he said. I had the feeling that he wished I would go away.

"I have to go over to Mrs. T.'s to return the book I borrowed," I told him. "I'll be back after a while. Maybe you'd better hang around here so Mom won't worry about you."

Something in his expression closed tightly. I recognized the look, having worn it a few times myself.

"Suit yourself," I said, giving in. "But if you go anywhere, maybe you'd better leave a note."

"Are *you* going to leave a note?" he asked.

"Not this time. Mom knows where I'll be. See you later."

He nodded and closed the door as soon as I turned away. As I was going downstairs, I thought I heard it lock, but that could have been my imagingation.

Walking out of the house was like escaping from prison. It was all I could do not to break into a run, but I didn't. I held the books close to my side and sauntered across the street, in case anyone should be watching. The long shadows of the trees around Mrs. T.'s house drew me like welcoming arms. Through the open windows I could hear her playing the piano, the way she does when there's all the time in the world and she can get lost in it.

Home free, I thought as I went up the steps to the side deck and pressed the doorbell.

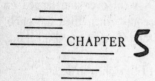

CHAPTER 5

The sun had gone down Friday evening when I came out of the back door of the church. The eastern sky was twilight gray, but a wide streak of gold light in the west held the day for a few minutes more. I felt tired and satisfied. It seemed to me that my music notebook actually gave off a warm glow, full as it was of my notes and ideas. I had tried them out and they sounded great, even on the church piano.

I stood for a moment or two listening to the evening noises and feeling somehow different. When I looked down at my feet, the ancient brick steps seemed farther away, like maybe I'd grown a few inches during the week. I couldn't help grinning as I fitted the key in the lock and tested the door. In terms of practice time, this hadn't been a bad week at all. I had managed an hour of practice in the church after dinner on Monday and Tuesday, and now again tonight. Except for Sunday afternoon I hadn't been to Mrs. T.'s. Twice Mom had asked, and I was able to say—without lying—that I hadn't. Maybe she would quit asking soon. Saturday had always been the day I looked forward to most because it allowed me a longer time at Mrs. T.'s to practice and to go over new music. Now, thanks to Mom, I had already missed one Saturday. I didn't intend to miss another, no matter what I had to do.

As I approached our house a few minutes later, I saw Georgie sitting on the top step, his knees knocked to form an inverted V, a prop for his elbows.

I came over and sat beside him, imitating his pose. "... you supposed to be getting ready for bed?"

"Maybe," he said, squirming. "I was going in if you didn't come pretty soon. I . . . didn't want to go in by myself."

"Oh? What's going on in there?"

"I don't know. I think Aileen did something bad." His eyes looked darker than ever in the fading light. His little face was screwed into a frown.

"Tell me," I said.

"Well," he said, inching close, "Dad is mad at her. She was coming downstairs and he took hold of her arm and pushed her. He yelled at her and made her go back up to her room. He called her bad names."

"Like what?"

"Lazy. Selfish. Useless. No-good."

I watched his face. I wondered what the congregation would think if they could hear the Reverend Richard Sloan call his daughter names. Maybe they wouldn't believe it. The person they see in the pulpit on Sunday, the man who visits the sick and shut-in, who counsels folks with problems, is certainly not the sort of man who would yell at his own daughter and push her upstairs.

"We'd better go inside before he or Mom come looking for us," I said. I picked up my notebook from the porch beside me and stood, rubbing my backside where I'd been sitting on the hard boards.

"Neal . . . "

The way he said my name made me brace myself.

"Neal, I like you."

For a few seconds there I didn't know whether I'd be able to swallow again. I was thankful for the dim light. "I like you too, Georgie," I muttered, giving him a playful punch on the arm.

If we had any ideas about getting upstairs without being noticed, they came to exactly nothing. As we passed the living room door, Mom called.

"Boys? Come in here, both of you."

He and I looked at each other. His chest rose and fell. I gave his shoulder a squeeze to let him know I'd take care of things, and I held the notebook so it would be as inconspicuous as possible.

She was folding clothes. Her hands reached, folded, smoothed in one motion. I had a sudden image of her doing that all night long, and to show for it in the morning dozens of stacks of clothes piled to the ceiling. She looked grim.

"Tomorrow's Saturday," she said. "What are your plans, Neal?"

"I promised Miss Patterson I'd mow her yard."

"I'm going over to Wayside in the morning. I thought you might like to go along," she said.

"I don't know." I hedged. "Maybe."

"Could I go?" asked Georgie.

She looked at him impatiently. "No, Georgie—I'll take you another time."

That decided it for me. Why *not* take him instead of me? Besides, I needed the time to practice. With Mom gone it would be easier for me to slip over to Mrs. T.'s and not have to answer questions about where I'd been. Still, it might be smart for me to wait until morning to tell her I wasn't going. Otherwise she'd lie awake all night dreaming up things to keep me busy till she got back from Wayside.

"Let me think about it," I said. "There are a couple of things I need to do here, homework and stuff—"

"I have something for you to do," Dad said suddenly from the doorway. "The churchyard needs mowing."

I thought about him pushing Aileen upstairs, yelling and calling her names, but there was nothing about his manner to suggest that anything disturbing had happened at all, or that he felt particularly sorry. He was so calm, so smooth. And he expected me to say, "Yes, sir!" Something in me resisted.

"I'll do it if I get paid," I said, "but not for free."

"I beg your pardon?"

"I'll do it for pay," I repeated, slowly and distinctly.

He took a step into the room. "I told Mr. McNally you'd do it."

I gazed back at him. I didn't say yes or no. Maybe because I didn't argue he thought it was settled his way.

"I'd advise you to go ahead and do your homework now," he went on. "You may not have time to get to it tomorrow. Mr. McNally may have other chores for you at the church."

Yeah, I'll bet, I thought. I remembered the time I'd washed eighteen stained glass windows for nothing except the "opportunity to serve." And ever since I've been old enough to run a mower, somehow the job has fallen to me. Everyone else pays me for mowing, but not the church—because my dad's the minister.

Georgie looked up at me, his eyes full of questions. I was afraid he'd start asking them aloud if I didn't get him out of the room.

"Excuse us," I muttered to no one in particular. "We'll go upstairs now. I'll see that Georgie gets to bed." I more or less herded him in front of me. It seemed to me that he shrank back as we passed Dad near the doorway.

"Good night, boys," Mom said. Her voice sounded softer, but maybe that was just by comparison with Dad's.

Later, when Georgie was in bed and I was just coming out of his room, the doorbell rang. I went to the banister and peered over to see who it might be. At the same time, Aileen came out of her room. Her eyes were red and swollen, and for just a second I thought she might turn around and go back. Instead she came over and looked, too. Mom opened the front door and switched on the porch light.

"Oh! Hello, Lola. What a nice surprise." I thought she didn't sound as though it were either nice or surprising for Lola Phifer to show up at this hour.

"I'm sorry to bother you," Miss Phifer apologized, "but I just didn't know who to turn to but Mr. Sloan."

"Of course—it's quite all right," Mom murmured. "I'll get him."

Aileen and I looked at each other, and I think we were both

wearing the same Oh-Lord-here-we-go-again face.

"I'm glad you felt free to come by." Dad's voice was deep and comforting. You could almost lie down on it and take a nap. "Here, why don't you come into the study and tell me what . . . "

The door closed behind them. Aileen's eyes rolled up and she made an awful face.

"God bless you, dear Miss Phifer," she said, close to my ear, imitating Dad's public tones. "Shall we pray about it?"

I don't know—it struck me funny somehow, and I nearly choked trying to keep quiet. Mom has ears like a fox. I leaned against the door to my room, doubled over laughing.

"It's not *that* funny," Aileen said.

"I think it's funny!" I snorted.

But then all of a sudden it wasn't. It was more like I was laughing to keep from crying or yelling. The yells I'd always held back were really there after all, floating around in the atmosphere. I had the weird feeling that if I closed my eyes and listened I'd be able to hear them.

"Hey!" said Aileen. "Take it easy!"

Why is she saying that? I wondered. Then I realized my face was wet.

"Come in here." She took me by the arm and pulled me into her room. "This seems to be the night for it." Her voice was dry as leaves, and matter-of-fact.

"He makes me so goddam mad!" I yanked a pillow from a chair and punched the daylights out of it. I wheeled around and caught her staring at me.

"You, too?" she said. "I thought you were on his side."

"Why the hell did you think that?"

She shrugged and sat down on the bed. "You never rock the boat. You don't do anything that'll make him mad at you."

"A person has to survive. What's the use of declaring open warfare? All it does is leave you battered and him on guard. *You* sure ought to know that."

"I know it, all right. I also know if I kept my mouth shut I'd die from the dishonesty of it."

"Georgie tells me Dad got rough with you tonight," I said.

She looked away. "If he ever lays a hand on me again, I'm going to do something awful."

"Like what?"

"Get him where it hurts the most—in his reputation. People think he's wonderful. We're the only ones who know otherwise. Keeping it from them has made *us* into weirdos. I wonder sometimes how he would be if he didn't have us to criticize and bully."

I felt sick to my stomach. "He wasn't always like this, was he, Aileen? Maybe he's just gotten this way in his old age."

"Are you looking for excuses for him, too?" she said coldly. "Don't you see where it puts us, the rest of the family? People would rather believe there's something wrong with *me*. They'd rather believe that poor Mr. Sloan prevails in spite of his sharp-tongued, unfriendly wife. His wild daughter. His strange, lying little boy!"

She stopped and looked at me. Her tone changed to faintly mocking. "They'd probably say you were the only normal person in the family. 'A nice young man. Maybe he'll grow up to be a minister, like his dad.'"

"Shut up!" I said. "I'd rather die!"

"I've wondered about you," she said, leaning back against the headboard. "I've wondered how you could let Dad run on without saying anything, ever."

"Look—people handle their lives whatever way they can. If you want to be the great, all-time revolutionary, then that's your business. I don't. I'm saving my energy for m—for something else."

"Do you remember when you came in here last weekend and suggested I knuckle under and do right?" she said. "Believe me, I want to 'do right,' but I want to do it for my own reasons, not just to preserve Dad's fine reputation. I don't want to have to die of shame if I fail at something I try. I want to be a real person, not just somebody's idea of what a preacher's daughter is supposed to be like!"

I went to her front window and looked out over the porch roof. Beyond was the street and the dark outline of Mrs. T.'s house. Through the window I glimpsed a light burning, probably the piano light. She would be playing the piano, as she often did at night. I ached to be there, listening.

"Yeah," I said. "I know what you mean."

My chest felt heavy, sore. One of the reasons I'd been able to take Dad's heavy-handedness these past two years was knowing I had an escape hatch. What went on here in this house had never seemed as real to me as what was there, across the street. Now that I couldn't go there whenever I liked, I knew that what happened here was going to matter to me more.

I turned back from the window and sat on the ruffled dressing table bench. "You make me feel guilty for not speaking up when Dad gets on your case."

"I can't make you feel guilty—guilt makes you feel guilty."

"I think I'm doing the right thing. I've got to be here a long time. No doubt I'll get what's coming to me after you're gone."

"Probably." She looked at me with something approaching affection. "As you say, people have to handle their lives whatever way they can."

"Were you going out with Pete tonight when Dad stopped you?"

Her eyes dropped. "Yes—and I didn't lie about it, either."

She got up from the bed and moved over to the mirror, touching with her fingertips the puffiness under her eyes. "I know what you're thinking. You think that if he really cared anything for me he'd be here in a flash to see if something had happened to me, or that at the very least he'd call. But why should he be insulted—"

She stopped in midsentence, picked up a brush and began brushing her hair. I had the feeling I was being dismissed.

I stood up. "I'm not making any promises I'll be different."

She gave me a mischievous, sidelong look. "I'm not, either."

Later, in bed, I lay awake a long time, thinking. Just before dropping off to sleep, I made up my mind. In the morning I was going straight to Mr. Mac and tell him I'd mow the churchyard for eight dollars. If he didn't want to pay me, he could get somebody else who would do it for nothing. It was between me and him.

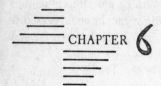

CHAPTER 6

I woke up to Mom standing next to the bed calling my name.

"Neal, I'm leaving in thirty minutes. Are you going or not?"

For a few seconds I couldn't think what she was talking about, then I remembered she'd invited me to go to Wayside with her.

"I don't want to go," I mumbled into the pillow without opening my eyes. "Take Georgie. He'd like it."

She didn't reply, but I could feel her still standing beside the bed. I could even imagine the exasperated expression on her face, but I knew better than to open my eyes to see if I'd guessed right. In a little bit she went out, leaving the door ajar.

And I couldn't go back to sleep. Believe me, I tried—it's awful to ruin a perfectly good Saturday morning waking up too early. But after a while I realized I was using more energy keeping my eyes closed than it would take to get out of bed. Still, I waited, listening for the sound of our car pulling out the driveway. The minutes stretched. My stomach growled. The house seemed un- usually quiet, even for a Saturday.

Then I heard voices in the downstairs hall. "Do you have your money?"

"No, ma'am," said Georgie. "I'm not going to take any."

"Well, I hope you've thought that through. Suppose you see something you want?"

There was a brief silence, then Georgie said, "I'll just look at it, I guess."

"I guess you will, because I'm not going to buy it for you."

"No, ma'am." The front door opened and closed, and soon they drove away. Part of me felt guilty—going to Wayside with Mom would have been a way to please her. But at least this way Georgie would have some fun for a change. I hoped.

I dressed and went down in my sock feet, ate a bowl of cereal, and thanked my lucky stars Dad wasn't around to test my resolve. By eight-thirty I was on my way out the back door. The sooner I finished the business with Mr. McNally, the better.

The closer I got to Mr. Mac's house, the more nervous I became. I rehearsed my speech.

Mr. Mac, Dad said you wanted me to mow the churchyard. I want eight dollars for the job. If you don't intend to pay, you'd better get someone else.

I thought about it some more. Maybe that was too harsh.

Mr. Mac, Dad said you wanted me to mow the churchyard today, but I can't do it. You'd better get someone else.

That was better. It didn't say *why* I couldn't do the job, but that was none of his business.

I went up the gravel path to the little white house where the McNallys live. You'd think that the man who owns most of the property in Gideon would have a bigger house, but I suppose one of the best ways to get rich is not to spend any money. I raised my fist to knock, but before I had a chance, the door opened inward and there stood Mr. Mac himself, in the act of putting on his battered felt work hat.

I opened my fist and lowered my arm, feeling foolish. "Er . . . good morning, Mr. Mac."

" 'Morning, Neal." He looked at me over his glasses. I noticed the gap between buttons just where his yellow shirt hung over his belt. "What can I do for you?"

"Well . . . I . . . wanted to tell you I can't mow the church-yard today so you'd better get someone else."

"Oh? Going out of town?"

"No, sir. I . . . uh . . . have another job."

He studied me for a moment, wiping a hand along his jaw.

Then he came out on the porch. "No time left to mow the churchyard?"

Moment of truth. Now or never. I swallowed. "Not for free, sir."

The words had come out of my mouth. I heard them with my own ears. So did Mr. Mac. His neck stiffened. "Beg pardon?"

"I'm trying to earn money for a . . . uh . . . special project," I said, wondering in amazement where that idea had come from. "From now on, every job I take will have to be for pay."

I stood there waiting for him to say something else. When he didn't, I began backing down the steps.

"I just wanted you to know," I said. "See you later."

I turned and walked down the path to the sidewalk, half expecting him to call me back. I looked over my shoulder once. He was still gazing after me.

My spirits rose with every step I took. Who would have thought that saying no could be so easy? I flexed my fingers, feeling the strength in them. It was hard to keep from grinning.

With Mom and Georgie gone and Aileen still sleeping it shouldn't be any problem to sneak back into the house, get my music books, and be gone again. I was burning to get to the piano before any more time passed. Inside, I took the stairs two at a time. My right foot was on the tenth step when Dad came out of the study.

He didn't see me at first. Maybe if I'd kept on going he'd never have known I was there, but fear can make a person do stupid things.

"Hi, Dad!" My voice sounded falsely cheerful even to me.

"What are you doing here?" he asked.

"I live here . . . remember?" It was supposed to be a joke. Dad scowled and looked at his watch.

"You're supposed to be mowing the churchyard."

This must be what it's like to step into quicksand unawares, I thought. You don't have time to think about what you're going to do before it happens.

"I've already been to talk to Mr. Mac about that." I took another step upward, testing my ground.

"Well—when are you going to do it?"

"I'm not. Mr. Mac's going to get someone else." One more step.

"Why is he doing that?"

I had reached the top by that time and had to bend a little, to be able to see him from where I stood. "Because I told him I wanted to be paid for the job."

Silence swirled around us and climbed until I feared we would drown in it. At last he spoke.

"I told him that you would mow the churchyard."

"But I didn't say I would. I said I'd mow it for pay. I didn't get an offer from either you or Mr. Mac, so I'm not mowing it. But it's no big deal—somebody'll be happy to do it for nothing, at least once. Mr. Mac will work his magic and—"

"That's enough!"

We went back to silence. I thought about the music books in the back of the desk drawer and replayed the past ten minutes of my life, wondering how I might have done things differently. I could see the door to Aileen's room from my position on the stairs, and wondered if she was behind it listening. Maybe she was gloating. I'd boxed myself in for sure this time, unless I took the offensive.

"Dad," I said, "it's all settled. I have another job which I'm about to do as soon as I change into my other shoes, if you'll please excuse me."

I turned and went to my room, closing the door firmly behind me. Some little-boy part of me fully expected to hear his footsteps thundering up the stairs in pursuit, but nothing happened. My heart was pounding so hard I had trouble breathing.

Change of plans. I pulled off my sneakers without untying them and put on the old grass-stained ones that I use for mowing. Miss Patterson's yard would have to be done before practice, dammit!

One thing was certain, I wasn't coming back here before nightfall. I got my knapsack out of the closet and stashed the music books and notebook in it. I put a clean pair of socks and my good sneakers in as well—no need to get grass stains all over Mrs. T.'s house. One last look around and I went out, turning the doorknob gently so it wouldn't squeal.

Dad was not standing there waiting for me. The study door was closed once more, so I kept going, right on outside to the street, cutting a diagonal across to Miss Patterson's.

She answered my knock so promptly that I suspect she was already standing at the front door peering through the curtains at whatever might be going on. She is plump, like a freshly boiled prune. She has pinkish blond hair and wears frilly blouses.

"Well," she said with a little explosion of breath, "I was about to give up on you, Neal! I just called your house about thirty minutes ago and your Dad said you were mowing the churchyard. I thought you'd forgotten about me."

I mumbled something about a mistake.

"The mower's in the garage," she went on, not really listening. "Keep track of your time."

That's a joke. She pretends to pay me by the hour, but she really pays by the job, usually with a little wad of dollar bills slightly damp from being held in her hand overlong. It's O.K., though, because the yard is flat and even, and I use her mower and gasoline.

I hung the knapsack on a limb of the pecan tree. When I came out of the garage, Miss Patterson had settled herself in a porch rocker. She had a Harlequin romance in her lap, but that was only for show. She's like an outdoor TV camera—anything that happens on our street in broad daylight is seen by her. You can count on it. I've often wondered why they don't put her in Gideon Bank and Trust—you know, hang her up in a corner in case the bank is robbed or something. Because not only does she see all, she tells all. If you don't want it known, don't do it on Water Street.

The roar of the mower engine blocked out all other sounds except the ones inside my head. I hummed to myself and couldn't hear a thing, but I knew what it was supposed to sound like. I hummed to keep alive the threads of music that had come to me earlier, hating that so much time had to pass before I could try it out. If only I hadn't gone back to the house. If only Dad hadn't caught me on the stairs. If I could have waited to mow Miss Patterson's yard this afternoon. My hands vibrated on the mower handle—they should be on a keyboard instead.

I finished in record time. Miss Patterson commented about it.

"My goodness, Neal—I'll have to sit out and watch you more often! Save myself some money. Are you sure you did around the rose bushes?"

"Yes, ma'am. But maybe you'd better inspect, just to be sure." I knew she couldn't find fault.

"I'll take your word for it," she said, dropping the damp wad of bills into my palm. "Gracious, boy, you do have big hands! Why, it doesn't seem any time since you were just a little squirt. You remember measuring your hand against mine when you were four?"

"No, ma'am." My face got warm.

"Well, you did. And you said you couldn't wait till your fingers were as long as mine. And now look!"

She held out a hand, palm down. For a plump person, she does have kind of slender fingers. The nails are painted pink and curve slightly upward, like the arch of a diver's back.

"Put your hand next to mine. See there? Mine is just *eensie* by comparison."

I definitely did not like comparing hands with Miss Patterson. It was embarrassing, not the sort of thing a guy would want his friends to see if he valued his future. I took my hand back and made a big deal of smoothing out the five ones and putting them in my wallet. My hands felt like they belonged to a giant. I don't know, I guess I've assumed they were invisible to everyone but me—or hoped they were. Now suddenly they felt like the most obvious thing about me, and I wondered if it was possible for people to tell by looking at them that I played the piano.

"Well, thanks," I said. I put the wallet in my back pocket and patted it in place. "See you in church tomorrow."

I pulled the knapsack from the pecan tree limb and departed under her watchful eye. Once again, though, I couldn't go directly to Mrs. T.'s, because sooner or later Mom would find out about it from Miss Patterson.

Obstacles. Why is it that when I know what I want things come out of the woodwork to keep me from getting it?

My stomach made growling noises, reminding me that lunchtime had arrived and that I couldn't go home to fill it. Fifteen minutes later I was at Bailey's buying a chicken salad sandwich and an R.C. Bailey's store is a good place to be on Saturday if you want to remain unnoticed. Lots of people come to town, and all the clerks are too busy to talk. I stood over at the side to eat, watching the activity with half an eye, but mostly thinking about how complicated life seemed to be getting.

"How do, Neal!" Mr. Bailey came up behind me and put a hand on my shoulder. He looks as though he were carved out of a cypress limb, all lean muscle and ruddy skin. "Haven't seen you in a few days!"

"School," I said, with my mouth full.

"Your little brother was in here one day last week."

"Yes," I said, "He told me."

"Everything O.K. at your house?"

"Sure!" I set the R.C. bottle in the crate by the drink box and threw the sandwich wrapping in the trash can, shifting my shoulders to relieve the pressure of the knapsack. Mr. Bailey's question bothered me.

"Glad to hear it," he said. He kept standing there looking at me. I felt like a fly pinned to a board. What did he want?

Then I remembered Georgie's arrangement with him. Ah ha! I pulled out my wallet and took the five ones, still damp, from the fold.

"Georgie told me you let him buy some stuff on credit," I said. "He shouldn't have done that. Dad wouldn't like it. Let me pay you what he owes and then he can pay me back."

"Nope!" Mr. Bailey put up a hand and shook his head. "I wouldn't think of it. He's a nice little fellow. He'll pay what he owes me. It ain't that much anyhow."

I put the money back in the wallet. "Georgie gets funny ideas sometimes. He has an overactive imagination."

Mr. Bailey frowned. He looked as though he wanted to say something but then thought better of it. Instead he patted me on the shoulder. "O.K. Well, you just let me know if I can be of any help."

"Sure. Thanks." I moved away from him toward the door. He nodded and turned to a customer. His words bounced around in my head. What a weird thing to say—like somebody in the family had died or something!

Outside again, I decided to take the back way to Mrs. T.'s house. It's possible to walk behind houses along the waterfront from one end of town to the other. It means skirting full clotheslines, garden plots, flower beds, and other backyard paraphernalia, but since I don't make a habit of wearing paths through people's yards, I figured I could get away with it this once. Miss Patterson wouldn't be looking in this direction.

I went down to the pier in back of the store and then crossed over to the path behind Beth's Gift Shop. You learn a lot about Gideon from back here. Where fronts of houses and businesses face the street, most everyone keeps up appearances, but from back here you can tell who is really neat and who is just putting on. Mr. Bailey's property is clean and uncluttered. Two doors away the gift shop, which is full of little knickknacks ladies like to buy, is a rat haven of weeds and discarded trash. I was picking my way around that when I heard someone call my name.

"Hey, Neal! Out here—on the river!"

Looking over my shoulder, I caught sight of Pete Cauthin about fifty feet from shore in a little two-for-a-nickel rowboat he found washed up after one of last year's hurricanes. He has an outboard motor on it that makes the bow stick up out of the water like the *Titanic* about to go down.

"Want a ride?"

I didn't, at least not with him. Still, I *could* get to Mrs. T.'s a lot faster by boat.

"Yeah!" I called, cupping my hands around my mouth. "Pick me up at the bowling alley pier!"

I scrambled down the bank, and in a couple of minutes he pulled alongside, holding the boat steady for me while I got in.

"What the hell you doin' back here?" he said. "Poison ivy, snakes, rats—"

"Just taking a shortcut," I said. He gunned the engine, tumbling me backward on the middle seat.

"Where are you going?" he asked.

"You can take me as far as Mrs. Talbot's."

He cocked his head to one side and looked at me. "You stay over to her house a lot, don't you?"

I didn't need that—not from him. Aileen has a big mouth! "No, not really. I do chores for her." I turned around on the seat so my back was to him.

"She's some good-lookin' woman—you ever seen her in a bikini? For an old lady she is put to-ge-ther!"

"Shut up!" I said.

"Wha—?"

"Shut up!"

"Well, what's the matter with you? I just paid the lady a compliment."

"It didn't sound like a compliment." I waited for him to toss me overboard, but maybe he was too surprised to do anything . . . yet . . . so I changed the subject quick.

"Where were you last night anyway?" I asked. "Didn't it bother you when Aileen never showed up?"

The silence that followed my question was so profound I looked around to see if he had heard me.

"She tell you to ask me that?"

"No. She didn't know I'd see you."

He turned the boat slightly so that we were heading out toward the middle of the river. "I'd tend to my own business if I was you," he said.

Was he ashamed? Angry? There was no way to tell. I figured I'd do myself a favor, now that we'd traded insults, and not initiate any more conversation. Even Steven. Just let me get to Mrs. T.'s pier.

"What's in the pack?" he asked suddenly.

The question caught me off guard. I'd almost forgotten the knapsack. "Just some stuff."

"Anything to eat?"

"Naw—shoes." It was partly true.

"Funny shape for shoes," he commented, leaning forward and reaching for the pack. Before I could move away from him, his large hand was patting the nylon. "By God, you got books in there! Keer*ist*, man! Hauling books around on Saturday?"

If Pete Cauthin found out they were music books, I might as well migrate to Alaska. When I shoved him, my hand slipped and caught him just under the chin. If he hadn't had to keep a hand on the motor handle, I think he would've come at me.

"What's with you anyhow, you little turd! You wanna get out?"

"All I want is to get to Mrs. Talbot's. If I'd known you were gonna make a federal case of it, I would've walked—"

"You should've done that," he said coolly. "What you in such a hurry to get to her house for? What y'all plannin' to do?"

I flipped. I stood up in the boat, my legs apart for balance, and roared. "Goddammit, Pete, I'm sick of your shit!"

"Siddown, stupid—you're gonna fall out! And watch your language—don't you know how sound carries over water? If your dad and the church people hear you, you'll be on ice for weeks!"

He was laughing at me. I couldn't even see him any more. I reached over and grabbed a wad of T-shirt with one hand and pushed his oily face backward with the other. The boat veered as his hand slipped off the steering mechanism, and the next minute we were struggling and sputtering in the cold water over our heads. When we surfaced, spitting river, the boat was moving slowly away from us.

"Now look what you've gone and done, bonehead! I hope somebody shoots me if I ever do you a favor again!" He lunged away from me and started swimming toward the boat, which was moving in the direction of the shore, but at a long angle. "Come on, jackass—help me catch it!"

To hell with you, I thought, striking out for Mrs. T.'s pier. The knapsack had slipped around and was weighing me down. All I could think about was getting out of the water before the books got soaked.

It took several minutes of swimming to get to water shallow enough to put my feet on bottom, and another couple of minutes to reach the end of the pier. I hauled myself up, waterlogged and chilled, in time to see Pete's boat ram Mrs. Burney's pier several houses away.

Now what? I thought, shivering in the sharp wind coming off the river. The splintery boards were warm from the sun, and I lay there for a minute, pressed against them, as water ran off my clothes and dripped down between the cracks. I didn't want to think about what this little incident would mean. Pete Cauthin is not a person anyone would want for a declared enemy. If only I hadn't accepted his offer of a ride.

I got to my knees, thinking how there had been an awful lot of ifs in the day and it wasn't over yet. I slipped the soaking knapsack off my shoulder and tried to undo the knot, but it was too wet and my hands were shaking from the cold.

The best thing to do was to get inside out of the wind. Mrs. T. would lend me a towel. As I climbed the steep bank to her rear deck, I felt as though I weighed three hundred pounds. It was like the end of a bad dream—one of those where you try and try to get to a certain destination but you never reach it because things keep getting in the way. I pounded on the back door and waited, leaning against the sun-warmed wall for comfort.

No one came. The brass knob didn't turn when I tried it.

Sometimes she leaves the side door open when she's going to be gone for a while, so I can get in to the piano. I went around, opened the screen, and turned the knob. It wouldn't budge. She had locked me out!

I kicked at the heavy door with my sodden shoes, then rammed it with my shoulder like some kind of nut. By that time I was shaking so I couldn't stand up. I sank to the deck with my back against the door and my knees drawn up against my body. Again I fumbled with the wet knot on the knapsack. After an eternity the knot finally came free and I jerked open the pack.

The music books were wrinkled, the pages clinging together. But that wasn't the worst. Water had smeared the ink on many of the notebook pages—my ideas, the ones I had tried and the ones I wanted to try, were nothing but a light blue blur. Weeks of work—gone!

I leaned my head far back and stared up through the trees with my mouth open but no noise coming out. The ache in my throat blocked the sound, but if it ever did break free it would be heard all the way to heaven. I cried with no sound, the hot blinding tears running into my mouth and falling on a shirt already so soaked it didn't matter any more.

CHAPTER 7

That's where Mrs. T. found me I don't know how much later, on the side deck, cold and wet and about half-crazy.

"Good God, Neal! What happened? Are you all right?" She squatted beside me and shook me hard. She had on a flannel shirt and jeans. She looked warm.

"I'm freezing," I said, through stiff lips.

"*Why* are you sitting here with wet clothes on?"

"You know, that's exactly what Mom would ask."

"Get up," she commanded. "We're going inside." She dug in her purse for the key and unlocked the door, holding it open for me. The afternoon sun poured in through the large windows. I went straight over and lay down on the floor in a patch of sunshine. I didn't think I'd ever be warm again. Shortly I felt the light fall of a blanket over me.

I listened with closed eyes as she moved about in the kitchen. She didn't talk. I recognized the familiar clunk of the teakettle on the burner. After a while she returned to the living room and pulled a chair over to where I lay.

"All right—what happened?"

I turned over and saw that she had my music books and the soggy manuscript paper in her lap and was blotting pages with paper towels. I put my arm over my eyes.

"Pete Cauthin is a dumb ass! He . . . said something that made me really mad. We got in a fight in his boat and fell overboard."

"He must've said something pretty terrible for you to fight him.

Not very many people would take him on. I've never known you to lose your temper like that."

It was true. It seemed to me that since last night the control I'd managed for years had begun to slip away. That scared me. Maybe this is the way people go crazy! I moved my arm and searched her face for clues. Did she think I was going crazy?

"You've got to get out of those wet clothes soon or you're going to be sick," she said. "You'd better go home and change. I'll dry the books in my oven."

I closed my eyes again.

I'll die if I have to go home. I don't want to talk about what happened. I hate life in that house with those people. It would suit me fine if I never had to see them again.

"Neal, did you hear?"

"Yes."

"Listen to me. Look at me and listen."

I opened my eyes. She leaned forward in the chair and looked down at me. "I know that you haven't had a chance to practice today, and that you've looked forward to your time here—but it wouldn't be very responsible of me to let you sit around in wet clothes. I have nothing here for you to put on. You must go home now. You can come back as soon as you change."

"Mom won't let me come back," I said stubbornly. "Neither will Dad. He's mad at me. If I leave now that'll be it for today—maybe for several days."

"Neal, remember our talk last week?"

"Sure I remember it!"

"If your folks knew you were coming here for music lessons or to practice, you wouldn't have to sneak around and pretend any more. It would be so much easier—"

"You don't know my folks very well, do you?" I interrupted. "Or anyone else in Gideon, for that matter. It wouldn't be easier, believe me!"

"Well," she said, "then it's time for you to think about the problem this creates for me."

I sat up, instantly on guard. "What problem?"

"You've asked me not to tell anyone that you are studying music with me. I never have, in the whole two years. Now that you're older, people are paying more attention to the fact that you stay here a good bit. Your mother is worried about it. Perhaps I would be worried, too, if I were her."

Anger flared in me like wildfire through dry brush. I leaped to my feet, hating my hot face and the remembered ugliness of Pete Cauthin's remarks in the boat. I wanted her to hush.

"I never thought I'd see the day that you'd be worried about gossip!" I choked. "Is that why you locked the door? You're no different from . . . from Dad!"

She stood up too. "That's not fair, Neal," she said gently. "You're my best, my favorite pupil. And you're my friend. I think you have a great future in music, but you can't keep it hidden forever. It's time you claimed your gift so that you can develop it. You can't be a jazz musician in a cave."

My chest seemed to harden as she spoke. I was turning to stone. When she stopped, the last word echoed and echoed—cave cave cave

"I guess that means I won't be using your piano any more, then," I said dully, "because I'm not telling. The timing is wrong."

"When will it be right? It takes so much less energy to live an honest life."

"Ha! I don't know anything about that—nobody's ever showed me how it's done. Here—give me the books."

"I was going to dry them—"

"Why bother? Sounds like I won't be using them much any more."

Tears sprang to her eyes, and she opened her mouth as though she meant to try again, but she changed her mind. Instead she handed me the wet books and the knapsack. I stuffed everything inside it.

"Be careful!" she warned. "Wet pages tear easily."

"What's the difference?" I muttered, and walked out of the house, slamming the door behind me.

For a few seconds I stood on the deck and looked across the street at our dumb house all tight and boxy, holding so much rot inside its trim brick corners. The car in the driveway meant that Mom and Georgie were back from Wayside. If I let myself think for one minute about what was there waiting for me, I wouldn't be able to cross the street. It was like getting ready to turn myself in at the prison gate or something.

I just quit thinking and went home.

This time I didn't try to sneak in or anything. From the hallway I could hear voices in the kitchen and the sound of hammering in the backyard. I was tensed for the battery of where-have-you's and why-didn't-you's, but they never happened because no one heard me come in. I went straight upstairs to my room and peeled off the wet clothes, leaving them in a pile on the floor. I tossed the knapsack under the bed—I didn't want to see it any more. After putting on a dry sweat suit, I climbed into the unmade bed and pulled the rumpled sheets up around my neck.

For a few seconds I managed not to think about anything except getting warm, but it didn't last long. Everything was so messed up. I couldn't believe Mrs. T. It just didn't make sense. It was like she was more worried about how things looked than she was about what happened to me.

And then it hit me. I sat straight up in bed.

Mom.

Instead of letting me take care of it, Mom had called Mrs. T. and made things ugly. As soon as I thought it, I was certain it was true.

It made me sick—literally. I threw up in the wastebasket. I was leaning over it, retching, when Mom came in without knocking.

"Neal—what's wrong? Are you sick?"

"No." I spit. "I'm just practicing throwing up."

"Get into bed." She picked up the wastebasket and started out of the room with it. I obeyed, not because she told me to but because I couldn't stand up too well. In a few minutes she was back with a glass of water in one hand and the wastebasket in the other. She handed the water to me and sat on the edge of the bed.

"You don't have a fever," she said, testing my forehead with a cold hand. "What did you have for lunch?"

"Doesn't matter." I took a sip of the water. "It's gone now."

"What's the matter with you, anyway?"

I looked her straight in the eye. "Why'd you do it?"

"Why did I do what?"

"Why did you meddle in something that was none of your business?"

"I don't know what you're talking about."

"I'd expect you to say that," I said bitterly, "but I wish to God you had the guts to be honest for a change!"

"You have no right to talk to me that way!" Her low voice trembled. "At least quit speaking riddles and tell me what you mean."

"You know what I mean. You talked to Mrs. Talbot, didn't you? You told her not to let me come over any more!"

She looked as though I'd slapped her. "No, I didn't!" she breathed. "I never did. You were supposed to take care of that."

And I knew she was telling the truth. If she'd done it, she would already be rationalizing, explaining to me why it was for the best and all. But she just sat there looking at me with dark eyes, hung up on the hurt of being unjustly accused.

"Then why . . . ?" But I couldn't even ask the question without giving away my secret.

She got up and turned away quickly. She saw the pile of wet clothes lying on the floor and bent over to pick them up. She didn't ask how they got wet.

"Is there anything in the pockets?"

"My wallet."

"Do I have your permission to remove it, or would you prefer to do it yourself?"

I got out of bed, shamed by her hurt, and went through the pockets of the jeans and shirt. "I'll wash these," I muttered. "You needn't bother."

"Suits me. Don't wait too long, though. They'll sour."

She went out, shutting the door firmly behind her. I sat on the edge of the bed, feeling colder than ever. The clock on the nightstand said four-thirty.

There was a light tap on the door. "Come in!" I said, pretty sure it was Georgie. Nobody else in the family would wait to be asked in.

He came in timidly, holding to the doorknob as though it were an escape hatch. He held the other hand behind him. "Mom said you were sick."

"Not any more. Something disagreed with me. I'm not contagious."

He let go of the doorknob and came farther into the room, somewhat like a baby rabbit in someone's garden, sniffing the air and expecting danger from every side.

"Here," he said, bringing out the hand from behind his back. "I brought you something."

It was a bag of salted peanuts. I smiled. "Thanks. That was thoughtful of you." I took the peanuts and tore open the bag. "You buy these in Wayside?"

"N-no. I already had them."

"Here—hold out your hand," I said.

Instead he put both hands behind him. "No. They're for you."

"I'll get sick if I don't share them," I said with a straight face. "You don't want me to be sick again, do you?"

"I don't believe that. You're teasing me."

"You're right—I am. But I do want you to have some of the peanuts—that's the truth."

He held out his palm then and let me pour some into it. I held my own hand cupped under his in case any spilled. His seemed very small. The nails were bitten to the quick, and I noticed again the slight tremor of his body. It is always hard for Georgie to do anything that requires fine coordination because his hands shake most of the time.

"Here," I said, patting the bed beside me. "Sit and tell me about your trip this morning."

He sat next to me as close as he could without actually touching. I think he's scared I'll knock him off into next week if he gets too close. "I wish you'd gone with us," he said.

"Well, you and Mom probably had more fun without me. Sometimes three's a crowd. What did you do?"

"First we went to the doctor's office. We had to sit a long time. He didn't have very good magazines, either."

I leaned down and looked him in the face. "What doctor? Who's sick?"

He stared back at me as though he were entertaining the question for the first time. "I don't know."

I was about to get impatient. "You don't know which doctor, or you don't know who's sick?"

"It was Dr. Koch."

Dr. Koch is our family doctor. "So? You sat and waited while Mom went in to see Dr. Koch?"

"Yes."

"Then what?"

"Then we went downtown shopping. Mom bought socks for Dad and a blouse for Aileen and—"

"Georgie, back up. Did Mom say why she went to see Dr. Koch?"

He shook his head. "She didn't act sick. She was thinking about something, though, because she didn't listen to me sometimes."

I pondered. Sometimes you go to doctors for things that don't show. Sometimes the things that don't show can be worse than those that do. Would she have gone if I had been with her instead of Georgie? Was that why she asked me in the first place?

"You look funny," Georgie said.

"Maybe I'm getting sick again," I mumbled. Then when he

got all worried, I had to backtrack and assure him that I wouldn't be sick before his very eyes.

"Dad told Mom that you didn't mow the churchyard," he said, changing the subject. He actually beamed.

"That's right," I said, "but don't you get any big ideas about defying Dad because of that, you hear me?"

His smile faded. I'd read his mind.

"I can get away with it because I'm fifteen and as tall as he is. You're too little." Besides, I thought, I may not have gotten away with it really.

He looked down at his hands, busied himself picking imaginary lint from his pants. "I can't wait that long," he said.

I wasn't sure I'd heard him right. "What did you say?"

"I can't wait till I get as big as you." He looked up at me, and his face was like that of an old person, full of pain and desperation. It shook me up. It seemed like he had gone to another level and left me behind—we weren't talking about the same thing any more.

I put my arm around him—or rather, it was like my arm put itself around him, almost a reflex, like reaching out to grab a balloon that's about to fly away.

"Georgie, it's hard times." I scrambled for words. "Things will be better."

He stood up suddenly, and my arm slipped off his shoulder. "I have to go now."

"Where?" I asked.

"Different places," he said vaguely. I thought as I watched him leave that he was almost like a cloud of mist. His footsteps made hardly a sound.

Somehow his being there got me out of the dirty wallows. I made up the bed to keep from getting in it again, then got down on all fours and pulled the knapsack out from under it. The dust woollies had caked themselves nicely on the damp nylon. One by one I drew out the contents: A wet sneaker. Another wet sneaker. Socks. Farley's *Rudiments of Jazz*. A book of finger exercises. *Theory for Intermediates*. And finally the notebook, its pages looking like watercolored skyscape. Mrs. T. had left in the books the few sheets of paper towels she'd used for blotting. I felt the pages. They were already nearly dry.

Mom probably wouldn't be too keen on my using a whole roll of paper towels, especially if I didn't tell her why I needed it. I shoved all the stuff back under the bed, picked up the pile of wet clothes, and went down to look for some old newspapers for blotting.

"Feeling better?" Mom asked as I went through the kitchen. She was stirring something that smelled like beef stew.

"Yes." I started to walk on by, but I couldn't do it. "And I'm sorry about what I said a while ago. I should've checked my facts before I started spouting off."

"It's all right," she said, not looking at me. I couldn't tell whether it was really all right or not. Probably we'd have to talk about it some more later. At least I could make amends by putting the river-soaked clothes in the washer instead of leaving it for her to do.

Dad was out in the backyard shed where we store old papers, sawing away on a board. He is always building bookcases for his study. When his books fill up all the available shelf space and start piling up on the floor, he builds another bookcase. At the rate he's going he'll soon have to build another study.

"Well," he said when I walked into the shed. "The Prodigal has returned."

I didn't think he meant for me to reply to that, so I didn't. I went over to the pile of papers in the corner.

"Have you wasted your substance in riotous living?" he went on.

"No, sir." Maybe he thought he was being funny, spouting Scripture. I picked up an armload of papers and started to leave.

He straightened, the saw dangling from his hand. Specks of sawdust were suspended in the little webs of hair that frizzed around his face.

"I don't suppose you're coming to apologize."

"For what?"

"For putting me in an embarrassing and awkward position—"

"Dad, I didn't put you in an awkward position—*you* did it. Ask me next time before you make promises about what I'll do."

"What's gotten into you, Neal? You're so arrogant all of a sudden. You have to remember that in a household such as ours, a person can't make selfish, independent decisions. *Other* people are involved!"

I looked at him hard, to see if he had any idea what he was saying. Was he listening to himself at all?

"Understand, it's not just me the people look at. What you and your brother and sister do comes under scrutiny too."

"You're telling me!" I muttered.

"You know," he said, propping a foot on the sawhorse and leaning forward, "it's probably hard for you to realize what being a minister in a town like Gideon means—how it affects the way a person has to live. A person has to give up a great deal."

"Yeah," I said, "but why does his whole family have to get roped in?" My voice, loud and flat, jarred him. He looked at me blankly, as though for a minute he'd forgotten his real audience was me—Neal—his son of fifteen years.

"Well . . . because. People expect certain things. They complain . . . or threaten . . . if those expectations aren't met. It can make life extremely difficult."

"I know about that," I said. "But how can you stand it, being miserable all the time, worrying about what people think? What's the good of it? If it was me, I'd quit." I shifted the papers in my arms and started again to walk out.

"Ha! That's easy for you to say. How can I quit when—"

He bit off the end of the word the way you'd chop a snake's head with a sharp hoe. The expression in his eyes was more desperation than anger. For that split second he seemed like a real person, not an actor. Then he turned away quickly to the board he'd been sawing.

"Never mind." He dismissed me. I went across the yard slowly, his words ringing in my ears. *How can I quit when—?* What was the end of the question?

Much later, with the door to my room locked, I carefully blotted every page of each music book between sheets of newspaper. The musical ideas I'd jotted down were pretty much beyond reclaiming, except for a page here and there. It felt like I was going to have to be born all over again—a grim prospect if I thought about it too much.

I couldn't count on Mrs. T.'s house, her piano, or maybe even Mrs. T. It was either give up my dream or find a different way to do it.

CHAPTER 8

It seems to me that Sundays happen every other day around here. About the time I get one of them out of my system, another rolls around. I pulled my usual trick of trailing behind Mom and Georgie, but this time it didn't work. She sent him on ahead and waited for me to catch up.

"Neal, *please* hurry up!"

"I'm coming, dammit!" I muttered.

I didn't think she heard me, but when we had walked a little way she said, "You'll have to watch your language."

"Why?" I said, playing it tough. "Will I get struck by lightning?"

"No—but your dad might." She laughed a little. "A bolt in the form of Mrs. Burney, maybe."

Mrs. Burney is one church member who is full of suggestions and criticism. I looked at Mom sideways, studying her pale profile for clues. I hadn't heard her make a joke in a long time.

"You know," I said, testing her, "it's a bitch being a preacher's kid. A person always has to do the right things for somebody else's reasons."

She looked straight at me. "I'll tell you something else. It's a bitch being a preacher's wife, too."

My eyes bugged.

"W-well," I said when I found my voice, "at least you had some choice in the matter. You weren't *born* to it."

"True. There is that difference, even though a person might make a choice before all the facts are in. Or they might make it on the basis of some assumptions that turn out not to be valid. Still, once the choice is made, it's a good thing to stick with it."

"Why?"

"Well . . . because. If people are forever deciding they don't like what they've chosen and throw it away or give it up and walk away, then . . . there wouldn't be any stability. You couldn't count on anything."

"Yes, but what if you take one road," I argued, "and when you've gotten about a mile along you realize you need to be on another road instead. Do you keep on traveling anyhow, even if it takes you miles and miles from where you need to be?"

"It's hardly ever that clear," she said.

It seemed to me she was about half right and about half wrong. I thought of the conversation in the shed with Dad, all the stuff about what he'd given up to be a minister. It seemed so dumb for people to be unhappy because they'd made up their minds to stick with their choice no matter what.

"What did you think it was going to be like when you married Dad?" I asked curiously.

She hesitated. "I was determined to be the perfect minister's wife. I would do everything that was expected because I wanted him to be proud of me and I wanted the congregations to be satisfied."

Just hearing it made me feel tired. "How long did *that* last?"

She measured me with her eyes, maybe to see how much more I could take. "I don't suppose I've ever given up trying, but I've never measured up."

"Who could?" I asked. "It's unreal for regular human beings."

"I've about come to that conclusion myself," she said, nodding. We had reached the church by that time, but more than ever now I didn't want to go inside. I was numbed by Mom's frankness. It was as if I had accidentally opened a closet and caught a glimpse of something I wasn't supposed to see yet.

"Don't be late for your class," she said, clicking into the old phrase automatically, the result of years of doing right. "It wouldn't look good for you to be the last to straggle in."

She walked briskly up the stairs and left me standing there trying to get straight in my mind the two people she had become. One was the ever-predictable person who said the same things every day and pushed us to conform. The other was this new person who had feelings and wasn't absolutely certain about herself—or anything else, for that matter.

I started down the hall toward the Sunday school room, but then stopped. If I didn't want to be in the stupid class, why did I have to? Once in a while a person ought to be able to do things for his own reasons. I turned around and went back outside.

The cemetery behind the church seemed the most likely spot to avoid company on such a fine morning. I made my way around the side of the building, walking purposefully in case anyone might happen to look out a window. Once I'd gotten to the far side of the cemetery, no one would be able to see me through the trees.

Because I was looking back over my shoulder, I didn't see Aileen until I almost stumbled over her feet. She was sitting on a large, flat gravestone that said "McNally."

"I wondered when you'd notice," she said dryly, grinning at my startled look. "If I'd been a vampire you'd be a goner by now."

"What're *you* doing here?"

"I could ask you the same thing, but I expect we have the same reason—Mr. Lakeland."

"What will he think, with both of us absent?" I asked, sitting beside her.

"Who cares? Maybe he'll send out a search party. They can act out the parable of the lost sheep."

We listened to the chirp of birds. Insects buzzed in the grass. I could even hear my own breathing. I began to think I might tell Aileen what Mom and I had talked about. It would probably make things between them a little easier.

"I think you ought to know"—Aileen interrupted my thoughts—"Pete's meeting me here."

I wasn't prepared for the surge of angry feeling at the mention of his name. Yesterday's trouble came back in a rush.

"Then I'm leaving." I stood up and brushed the seat of my pants. "I don't want to see the S O B."

"Wha-a-at? That doesn't sound like you, Neal. What's Pete ever done to you?"

"We got in a fight yesterday," I mumbled. "You'll hear about it."

"You got in a fight with *Pete*? But . . . why?"

"He said something I didn't like."

"It must've been pretty awful to make *you* fight! Who won?"

"I don't guess anybody did."

"Yeah," said a familiar voice from the edge of the cemetery, "I don't guess anybody did. Maybe we need a rematch."

Pete came striding toward us in jeans and T-shirt, picking his way around graves and patches of flowers. Aileen got up from her tombstone seat, all smiles, but he ignored her and ambled over to me. His right hand was clenched into a large fist. He tapped me lightly on the shoulder with it.

"My boat's scraped pretty bad," he said. "And I got to pay Mrs. Burney to have one of the pilings on her pier repaired."

"So?"

"So don't you think you might offer a little financial help, since it was your fault?"

"What do you mean, my fault? If you'd kept your big mouth shut—"

"I said some words—just jokin' with you. Can I help it if you got no sense of humor? Words are nothin', but when you start destroyin' people's property—"

"What *is* this?" Aileen shouldered her way between us. "What's going on?"

"Your little brother is too damn self-righteous for his own good," Pete said. "He starts a fight, knocks me out of my boat, won't help me go after it, and . . . as you can hear . . . won't help pay for the damage. The hell of it is, when I tell Mrs. Burney that the preacher's son is just as responsible as I am, do you think she believes me for one minute? Of course not, because he never does anything wrong!"

"Neal, is this story true?" Aileen asked.

"If I told it, it would sound different," I said, trying to look Pete in the eye.

"O.K. then, tell it," she said. "Let's hear it from your point of view."

I swallowed. "He . . . said something about Mrs. Talbot he had no business saying. I wasn't going to sit there and let him get away with it."

"Is that all?"

"What do you mean—*all*! If he said something bad about you, wouldn't you want me to protest? You don't let people get away with telling lies on your friends. Just because he's used to beating up everybody who looks at him wrong is no reason—"

"Wait a minute." Aileen put a hand on my arm. "Who started the fight? Who actually struck the first blow?"

I looked down at my feet. An ant crawled busily over my right shoe.

"You'd think the preacher's son would know better than that, wouldn't you?" Pete asked.

"What does being the preacher's son have to do with it?" Aileen said, turning on him. I think he'd forgotten temporarily that we come from the same stock. Her words caught him off guard.

"Well, you'd think that he wouldn't just fly off the handle over nothin'. I mean, all that prayin' and Bible readin'—"

"Your dad's a barber," I said. "Do you cut hair?"

His face darkened, and he took a step toward me. I thought wearily that I must have some kind of death wish to keep taunting him.

"Look," Pete said, "I don't have to stand around and listen to this shit. I'm just as good as you are, maybe better. At least I don't go around *pretendin'* to be good like some people!" He turned to Aileen. "I'm leavin'. You goin' with me or not?"

"I . . ." She looked uncertainly from him to me and back to him. "Do you want me to, Pete?"

He shrugged. "Suit yourself. My car's parked on Salton Street." He turned and strode through the trees the same way he had come. He didn't look back or beg.

The bright hair seemed out of place framing Aileen's sad face. In a minute or two we heard his Chevy's unmuffled engine erupt with a roar and go off down the street. In the quiet morning we could hear it for a long time.

"I'm sorry," I said.

"For what?" She tossed her hair back. Once again there was distance between us. She gave me a look I couldn't understand.

People began spilling out of the church doors suddenly, signaling the end of Sunday school. It was only a matter of time before someone would be asking where we'd been.

"I'm leaving," Aileen said, starting toward the trees. "If Mom wants to know where I am, tell her I've gone to the Catholic church."

"Are you really going there?"

"Why not? The show will be a lot better than the one here." In a moment she was gone. I looked longingly at the gap among the trees where she had disappeared. Why couldn't I leave, too?

Then I thought of Georgie sitting beside Mom in church all by himself. It wasn't fair. He was too little to do anything but obey. In the end I went into the sanctuary and sat next to him.

Mom leaned over and whispered, "Where's Aileen?"

"Catholic church," I whispered back.

Mom sighed and sat back. It was hard to tell whether the sigh was for Aileen or for herself. Maybe we should all go to the Catholic church, and then when Dad came out he'd see our empty pew. That should tell him something.

I don't remember too much about the sermon because I kept thinking beyond the words he was saying. Probably one of the reasons he's lasted so long in Gideon is his preaching—or his preaching voice. He knows how to make the words go up and down and when to be loud or soft. Those little tricks keep people's attention. About the time they're going to slide off into their own thoughts he blares out, or gets whispery, and they sit up, thinking they're going to hear something.

And maybe they do—I don't know.

It's just that living with him gives a person a different point of view. He is like the waterfront of Gideon—the part of him that faces the street is neat and tidy.

I looked at Georgie sitting next to me, his scrawny neck poking out of a shirt collar two sizes too large. The suit he wore was one I'd had when I was about five years old and it fitted him oddly, too big around and yet not long enough in places. I wondered if he noticed that he wasn't dressed like the other little guys his age and whether it mattered to him.

When we stood up for the benediction, Georgie took hold of my hand and turned his head so he could look up at me. I wondered idly how early he had discovered that God won't throw lightning bolts at you if you don't close your eyes when someone is praying out loud.

"Let's you and me head for home," I said in his ear as soon as the postlude started. I was not inclined to hang around—Mom and Dad would soon find out that Aileen and I had skipped Sunday school.

In the vestibule of the church Dad shook hands with people as they went out. I didn't want to shake his hand.

"We'll wait till Mrs. Burney comes up and then we'll go around," I told Georgie. We stood back and bided our time. Dad dreads to see her coming, but he has to stand there and listen. I figured that her customary complaints would give Georgie and me enough time to make a getaway. We edged forward as she did. I had my hand on his shoulder, and as soon as Mrs. Burney got to Dad, I steered Georgie around her and aimed for the front door.

Only this once Mrs. Burney didn't stop to deliver either tirade or commentary. Instead she gave him a little jerky handshake and moved on. She got out before we did.

"Well, boys—trying to sneak out?" Dad's voice said at our back, loud and clear for everyone to hear. Without even looking I could tell he was smiling, but I also knew the smile didn't get beyond his mouth.

Georgie looked up at me mutely, with a sort of what-do-we-do-now expression.

"You'd better not mess with that older boy." Mr. McNally had moved up and taken Dad's hand. "He's got a mind of his own."

Dad's smile stiffened. "Yes. Well, they do get like that when adolescence sets in. You know how it is."

Mr. Mac looked over and winked at me. It was, to my surprise, a friendly wink. "I guess," he said to Dad, "we're going to have to raise your salary some so you can support your family. Your boy's not able to work for free any more, as I understand it."

Dad was angry and embarrassed underneath the smiling countenance. I had seen it enough to recognize it. So had Georgie. I could feel him trembling next to me.

"Well, Neal and I had a communications mix-up," Dad said, trying to put the best face on things. "I don't think it will happen again."

"Don't get on him about it," Mr. Mac said mildly. "I kind of like the way he stood up for himself."

"Come over and shake hands, boys," Dad said when Mr. Mac moved toward the door.

We obeyed. Me first, feeling stupid and awkward under the eyes of all those people lined up to leave. Georgie next, putting out his small hand like someone about to have it severed at the wrist.

Look! I wanted to shout at everyone. *My little brother is afraid of him!*

But of course I didn't. The two of us went out the narrow door into the bright sunlight.

CHAPTER 9

We walked home in silence, Georgie trotting along beside me to keep up. When I finally realized I was going too fast for him, I slowed down to give him a breather.

"What will Dad do to us?" Georgie said after a while, voicing the question that had been marching in circles in my own brain ever since we left the church.

"Why should he do anything?" I said nonchalantly. "All we did was try to get out of shaking his hand."

Georgie didn't reply. We both knew that reasonableness had nothing to do with Dad's actions where we were concerned, especially lately. Add to that the fact that he must know by now that I'd played hooky from Sunday school. Somewhere else would be a good place to be when he and Mom got home.

"I have an idea," I said. "Let's make some sandwiches and take a picnic down to the landing."

"You mean you and me?"

"Sure! Who else?"

He smiled happily, but then just as quickly the smile faded and worry took its place. "Do you think it will be all right?"

I smiled back at him, but it felt sour and one-sided. "Probably not," I said, speaking honestly for a change. "But it ought to be. In any normal family it would be."

He looked at me in that quick way he has, as though he'd picked up something extra from my words.

"All right. We'll leave them a note," he said.

Within twenty minutes we had changed out of our Sunday suits, slapped together some sandwiches, grabbed a couple of apples and some cookies, stuffed them in my knapsack, and departed. My scribbled note said we'd be back in midafternoon. It did not say where we had gone.

"Captain Perry will let us eat on his boat," Georgie said. His face was brighter now. Every step he took away from the house seemed to lift some weight from his shoulders.

"Well, now, I don't know how Captain would feel about us inviting ourselves to lunch. He might have other plans."

"Captain Perry is always glad for me to come," Georgie said confidently. "He's my best friend."

Captain Perry must be in his seventies, and he's not a captain—that's his given name, like mine is Neal. He spent most of his life fishing for a living, going out into the sound every day and bringing his catch back to town to sell. Now that he's retired, no one pays much attention to him any more except my little brother. He doesn't have a tooth in his head, and because of a speech impediment it's hard to understand what he's saying. Georgie has no trouble, though. They carry on long conversations, but if you were to listen in you'd understand only Georgie's side. Captain's houseboat is a permanent fixture at the landing. He lives there year round, watching people come and go.

There were already lots of people at the landing when we got there, mostly the ones who hadn't gone to church. It was going to be a noisy day on the river with all those boats. The few picnic tables scattered about were already taken.

"Come on," said Georgie, motioning me to follow. This was his territory. He was in charge. We circled the crowd and came up on the left shore behind the spot where Captain moored his boat. Dragonflies skated over the river's surface. A stray gull squawked overhead. We stopped at the water's edge and Georgie cupped his hands around his mouth.

"Captain! It's me—Georgie. I've got my brother with me!" His overgrown voice echoed in the little cove. In a moment Captain appeared on deck a few feet away, waving his hand at us. His sunken smile was a gash in the lower half of his face. He called something in our direction. Georgie beamed.

"He says wait a minute and he'll put down the plank."

We waited while Captain struggled with the long double plank that served as a way to board the houseboat. He had nailed cross pieces along it to provide surer footing. He heaved it over the side, securing one end against the boat's rail. The bottom end was submerged in the shallow water. Captain called out something to us.

"He says to watch and not get our feet wet," Georgie interpreted. "I take a big step right over the water."

I followed him, marveling at how surefooted he seemed to be in this place. He scampered along the plank like a regular sailor, climbing over the rail with a quick flip of his skinny legs. I was more cautious. The tug of the knapsack straps on my shoulders reminded me of my cold baptism in the river the day before.

I had never been on board Captain's houseboat and was surprised at how trim and neat it was. It smelled warmly of the river—slightly fishy, partly wet, partly dry, and flavored with creosote.

Captain's smile had not diminished since he first caught sight of us. He mumbled some words, taking in both of us with his small blue eyes buried in crinkles.

"We brought a picnic," Georgie explained. "We brought enough for you, too, if you'd let us eat on your boat."

"Fine!" said Captain, only it came out sounding like "Vfa!" He waddled about on slightly bowed legs, pulling out deck chairs to sit in and a wooden crate to use as a table. Soon the three of us were munching away on the sandwiches, smiling self-consciously whenever we happened to catch one another's eye. Captain sort of gummed his sandwich. I was glad I'd put in cheese spread instead of ham or roast beef.

"Oo go shuh t'ay?" Captain asked.

"Yes," said Georgie, "but we didn't wait around afterward. We changed our clothes and fixed this lunch before Mom and Dad could even get home!"

"Oo te'm wheh oo ah?" Captain's face was serious now.

Georgie shot me a furtive glance. "No," he said. "We told 'em when we'd be back, though."

"Joge, ah toh oo nah do 'at!"

I heard the tone of reprimand in Captain's voice. In fact I was following his words O.K., now that I was really listening. He was talking like I do when I have a mouthful of toothpaste and need to spit. Apparently he had told Georgie never to go away without telling the folks where he was. Georgie looked very uncomfortable. He squirmed in the rickety deck chair.

"Neal said it would be all right," he said defensively.

"Yeah, I have to take the responsibility this time," I said. "I was the one who decided not to tell them where we were going."

Captain looked at me thoughtfully, as though trying to decide whether to go to the trouble of explaining something to me. I guessed what was behind the look.

"Georgie, Captain's right—it's not a good idea for you to go off alone without letting someone know. Something might happen to you."

I wasn't prepared for the look of fear that came into Georgie's eyes. He swallowed hard, and his Adam's apple went up and down. When he spoke, his voice sounded hoarse.

"What would happen to me?"

"*I* don't know," I said, irritated. When he gets scared it scares me, too. "But if you were playing near the river and fell in, or if you fell out of a tree and hurt yourself, nobody'd know for hours."

The anxious moment passed. We sat for a long time, watching the activity in the cove. It was very peaceful. The little houseboat bobbed gently in the ripples, once in a while plunging mildly as the wave from a speedboat's backwash reached us. I thought that this was what Sunday really should be like, calm and undemanding. The air was full of a kind of rough music—motors revving, little waves lapping, gulls mewling, splashes, shouting, the humming drone of boats far out on the river. I opened and closed my hands, feeling the ghosts of piano keys under my fingertips. The ache swept over me suddenly as it often did, but this time it seemed worse.

"It must be great to live here all the time," I said, making conversation to chase away the rising pain. At that point I would have discussed any topic anyone wanted to bring up.

Captain chuckled and shook his head. He began to talk. The words came steadily so that I had trouble following them. I looked to Georgie for help.

"He has plenty to worry about. Staying warm during the winter. Falling or getting hurt and nobody knowing it. Getting food— and being able to eat it once he gets it."

Georgie fell silent. Captain nodded, approving the translation.

"Have you ever thought about going into town to live?" I asked.

He shook his head and smiled. He said that sometimes he did, but that just thinking about it made him lonesome. He was not a land person. "Ah 'tay heh yong ez ah 'an," he finished.

"I could come live with you," Georgie said. "If anything happened to you I could go get help."

Captain laughed and tousled Georgie's hair. I saw that the old man really loved my little brother. It seemed too bad that Georgie didn't live with him. I was glad he had someone who cared about him that much.

Neither of us wanted to leave, but the note we'd left on the kitchen table was the same as a promise. I put what was left of wrappers and food back into the knapsack. "O.K., Georgie, it's time to go back now. Thanks, Captain, for letting us visit."

"An' 'ime," he said. We clambered along the plank to shore. Georgie turned and waved once, and Captain lifted an arm in response.

"Do you like Captain?" he asked when we'd gone a little way.

"Yes, I do. I didn't know what a neat person he was until today."

"He's my best friend," Georgie repeated, and I knew it was true. "I'm glad we went together. It was fun."

"Yeah. I thought so, too. We'll do it again."

"I wish we didn't have to go home," he said.

"Well, it's where we live. We just have to make the best of it."

"Neal, what did you mean when you said we weren't normal?"

I laughed. His questions always come at me from the side, and I have to laugh in self-defense. "Did I say that?"

"You know you did. It was on the way home from church. You said in any normal family it would be all right for you and me to go on a picnic."

"Well, it would."

"Then that means we're not normal."

"Look, Georgie, I don't know what normal is."

"Well," he said, "I do."

"Tell me."

He looked up at me, studying my face. I think he was trying to decide whether he could trust me to take him seriously.

"I believe normal is like we felt on Captain's boat. Not scared about everything."

I couldn't trust my voice to come out in one piece, so I just nodded. He reached and grabbed my arm just above the wrist.

"Neal, are you real?"

"Am I what? Well, sure—what do you mean, 'real'? I'm not a robot or an alien from outer space, if that's what you're getting at."

I peered into his eyes, trying to get to the bottom of his mind. It was like looking into a shifting cloud bank, yet I knew he was deadly serious.

"I mean, are you really Neal!"

"As far as I know, that's who I am . . . unless they found me on the doorstep when I was a baby—"

He tugged my arm impatiently. He had begun to tremble. "Don't tease!"

"Wait a second, fella." I put my hand on his shoulder. "I'm

not teasing. Come here—let's sit and talk a minute." I steered him over to the side of the street, and we sat on a grassy ditch bank in front of Mrs. Burney's house.

"All right now—what's all this about?"

He struggled for words. The twitching of his facial muscles was worse than usual. "I . . . *think* you are real," he said at last.

"Well, thanks—I think. What would I be if I wasn't real?"

Behind the thick glasses his eyes swam. "False," he whispered.

I waited. My own breathing sounded loud in my ears.

"I think Mom and Dad are False," he went on. "They are not our real Mom and Dad. And maybe Aileen, too, except Dad treats her so bad she might not be False after all."

I had two choices. I could laugh off the whole thing and tell him how silly he was, or I could hear him out. I kept my mouth shut and listened.

"For a long time," he said, "I didn't know if you were real or not. I couldn't ask, because if you were False—"

He stopped. The horror of his imagining was too much for him.

"Georgie, when did you start feeling Mom and Dad weren't your real parents?"

He frowned and looked down at the grass. "I don't know. I didn't think about it till this year, but after I thought about it, I decided they had been False a long, long time. Maybe since I was a baby."

"Do you mean you think you're adopted? At one time or another everybody thinks they're adopted—I did when I was your age."

"No." He shook his head. "Adopted is different. I think we were all living together, Real Mom and Dad, and Real Aileen and you and me. And then I think . . . I think . . . ." The words became difficult for him again.

"Do you think something happened to our real parents?"

He gave me a grateful look and nodded. "Somebody kidnapped them and took their place, secretly. It's like spies—how they can be anybody. Like they can change their looks so they are so much like the person nobody knows the difference." The words came faster now, tumbling over one another to get out. His voice was full of eerie excitement. It was creepy.

"Well, I have a question," I said. "Why haven't you and I been replaced?"

Immediately I saw in him the terror I'd seen flashes of during the past few days. He moved away from me a little. "I don't know," he said. "It could happen any day now."

I didn't know what to say. It was so real to him that I couldn't think of anything that would make it seem unreal. The bad thing was that if you looked at it from his point of view, you could see why he'd made up such a crazy idea. It's awful if you think your own parents don't love you, so you pretend they're not your real parents, and after a while what you pretend becomes real.

"I'll tell you what," I said carefully, standing up and brushing the seat of my jeans. "Maybe we should talk about this some more, later."

He leaped to his feet. "You're not going to tell!"

"No. You can count on that. I won't say a word. But I'm glad you told me, and I'm glad you decided I was real, because I am." I pulled him close as we walked along. "If we're going to be the only Real people in the family, we'd better stick together."

CHAPTER 10

As we walked back to the house, my mind raced, looking for an out. How bad off was Georgie? Should I just chalk it up to excessive imagination and hope he'd outgrow it, or was it really as bad as it seemed? The strange excitement in his voice and expression when he told his fear was scary. If he hadn't gone off the deep end yet, he seemed awfully close to it.

"You look mad," he said. "Are you mad at me?"

I realized that I had a fierce frown on my face. "No. But I don't want you to be scared all the time—it's not good for you. I guess I was thinking about how to keep you from being scared."

"Oh, I'm all right," he said. "I already—"

He stopped. "I'm all right," he finished.

There was so much about him that was hidden. Little pieces of him showed through to Captain probably, and to me, but mostly he was hidden. I tried to remember myself at his age. I don't think I spent a lot of energy hiding who I was then.

When we got to our yard, his hand came up and took mine in a kind of automatic gesture, the way you reach for something to hold onto when the vehicle you're in goes around a corner too fast

"It's O.K., Georgie," I said. "Nobody's going to do anything to you."

The front hallway was still, the way things are on Sunday afternoon—a nothing-is-happening kind of stillness. We might have been the only people alive. We went in on tiptoe.

"I'm going to my room," he whispered, nodding toward the stairs. "I'm sleepy." I watched as he went up, thinking maybe I could endure it if the house was quiet like this more often. But that was as hopeless as wishing the ocean waves would quit rolling in or that rain would fall up instead of down. Things are the way they are. I started upstairs, my mind on the music that lay in the drawer, wrinkled and smeared from yesterday's dunking. Even if I couldn't get to a piano, I could make some attempt to remember what I'd been writing down all these months. Then maybe tomorrow I could sneak into the church again and practice. I had to. This business of staying away from the piano was unnatural, like holding my breath or standing on my head. No one could do either of those things forever.

"Neal."

Mom's voice startled me, even though she spoke softly. She had materialized in the living room doorway as silently as Georgie.

"Can you come down a minute? I want to talk to you."

My heart sank, but I turned and went back down.

"Your father is taking a nap," she said. "Come with me."

I followed her through the kitchen and out to the back porch. She sat down on the top step, and I did too, wondering uneasily what this was all about.

"What happened this morning?" she asked.

"What happened about what?" I didn't intend to volunteer any information until I knew what she knew.

"Your father's pretty upset. All the way home he talked about your humiliating him in front of everyone and encouraging Georgie to defy him. He says he's been too lenient with you—that you're beginning to act like . . . Aileen. What brought it all on?"

My first impulse was to clam up, but there was something different in her tone—I didn't get the feeling that she wanted to trap me.

"Dad's still mad at me for not mowing the churchyard yesterday. I worked it out with Mr. Mac, and *he's* not upset at all—in fact, he'll probably pay me the next time he asks me to do a job.

But Dad acts like what I did made him look bad." I pulled a splinter from a porch board. "Shit! When I get up in the morning it makes him look bad, the way he acts!"

"O.K., calm down," Mom said. "How is that connected to this morning?"

I told her about Georgie and me leaving church, and how Dad had held up the line and made us both come back to shake his hand. "He did it because all those people were standing there," I finished, "to show us he was boss. Talk about humiliation! He was furious at us, but he kept smiling all the time. When Mr. Mac teased him a little bit about my not working for free any more, that did it."

She didn't say anything right away. She clasped her hands around her knees and rocked back and forth on the step, her forehead wrinkled in a deep frown. After a while she said, "Is that why you and Georgie went away and didn't say where you were going?"

"Yeah, mostly. Georgie was worried about what Dad might do to us. He stays scared of Dad, but he doesn't know what he's doing to make Dad angry. I thought if we could get away from the house for a while it might calm him down. Mom, why is Dad such a bully?"

She turned her head swiftly to look at me, as though my words had pulled all the breath out of her body. "That's overstating it a bit, don't you think?"

I shook my head. "A little guy shouldn't be scared of his own dad—not all the time."

She kept looking at me, trying to read what was in my brain. Finally she said, "Is he scared of me, too?"

"I don't know about that." I moved cautiously around the secret I'd promised not to tell. "He doesn't seem to be too sure about anyone any more, unless it's Captain Perry. That's where we were this afternoon."

"It's hard," she said, sighing. "One of the first things you learn about being a parent is that kids get mixed up if parents work against each other in matters of discipline. I've always tried to support Richard for that reason."

"Sure, you've supported *him*, but why doesn't it work the other way around? You're a pretty fair person. Why don't you take up for us when he gets so unreasonable?"

The silence lengthened. I had the feeling she was thinking of things she'd like to say, but then not saying them because it would be disloyal to Dad.

"Are you scared of Dad?" Even before the question had formed, it was already out of my mouth. At some level I must have been thinking it all along.

"Of course not! What a silly thing to say."

I was not convinced. If she was scared of him, what did she think he would do?

"Listen," she said hurriedly, "there's something you should know. Your father's under a lot of pressure right now. You shouldn't deliberately provoke him."

"Why is he under pressure? What kind of pressure?"

I waited while she made up her mind whether to tell, and how much. "You mustn't say anything about this to anyone—is that clear?"

"Sure, but if it's all that big, I'm not sure I want to know."

"Well, your father is fifty-six—not many years from retirement. He's been here in Gideon for fifteen years, a pretty long time to be in one place. He's been thinking about looking for another church—"

"Hot damn!" It burst out. Mom put a hand over my mouth.

"Hush! He'd be angry if he knew I'd told you. You must act as though you know nothing about it, understand?"

"But, Mom, that's crazy." I lowered my voice. "Why the secrecy? Hell! I've been wanting to leave Gideon for years. I think it's a great idea! Aileen will, too. If he needs some encouragement, we'll be glad to give it."

"You mustn't say a word—I mean it!" She seemed very nervous about having told me. "It's a risky thing for a person his age, in more ways than one. Suppose he puts out feelers and no one is interested in him? And of course there's the fear that he'll wear out his welcome here and the people will want him to leave."

"That might not be such a bad thing," I said callously. "Then he'd have to do something."

"Neal, that's unkind! You've no idea how frightening it is."

"I don't know what he's worried about anyway," I said. "These people think he can walk on water. As far as they're concerned, he's perfect. It's just his family they have problems with."

The pained expression on her face made me sorry I'd said it. We were back to the morning's conversation—our lack of perfection. "Mom, what do *you* want to do?"

"Whatever he wants to do, of course." She put up a hand and tucked back a strand of hair that had come loose. It sounded like a canned answer to me. I remembered all the times she complained because Aileen and I had to go to Gideon School where we aren't challenged to do our best. My mind flashed back to what Dad had said in the shed—how being a minister in a town like Gideon affects the way a person has to live. And I remembered my flip suggestion that he quit, and how desperate he'd looked.

"Who does he talk to?" I asked.

"No one—that's not his way."

"Well, dammit, how's he going to know—"

"Who?" said Dad behind us. Mom turned pale. Her brown eyes seemed suddenly too large for her face. I looked over my shoulder. He was standing just inside the screen door. I wondered how long he'd been there.

"Just a person I know," I said. "He has a problem."

"Oh." He came out on the porch. "Maybe I could help."

"It's no big deal," I said. "I don't really want to talk about it any more."

The color had come back into Mom's face. "I'm sorry we were talking so loud," she said. "We didn't mean to wake you up."

"You didn't. I decided to see if anyone else inhabited this house besides me." He looked at me pointedly. "When we came home after church, no one was here."

"I left a note."

"But you didn't say where you were."

"I said when we'd be back. Besides, how far can you go in Gideon?"

"Why didn't you go to your Sunday school class this morning?"

The swift accusation caught me off balance—I'd forgotten already. My only defense was to be honest. "Because I didn't want to."

"Neal, what in the world?" Mom sounded exasperated. I guess she thought she'd gotten me there safely when we parted ways in the hall of the church.

"Well, I didn't. Lakeland is a nerd. I thought I'd throw up if I had to sit and listen to him for an hour."

"And Aileen?" he said. "What's her excuse?"

"You'll have to ask her. We didn't collaborate, but we do feel the same way about Mr. Lakeland."

"Where is she now?"

"I haven't the foggiest," I said impatiently. "Don't worry—she'll be home after a while."

"I get the distinct feeling," Dad said, "that mutiny is going on right under my nose."

Well, I thought, that was downright perceptive of him.

"What I don't understand," he went on, "is why. It seems that anything I ask or expect is grounds for rebellion. What *is* it?"

"Richard, I don't think—" Mom began, but he waved an impatient hand.

"All I ask is a little reasonable cooperation from this family," he said. "You could make my work so much easier if you didn't try so hard to be different. It's not all that hard to behave like normal, respectable people. You don't *have* to create problems for yourself. I have responsibilities to an entire congregation—I can't just limit my concerns to the people in my own family."

Mom got up, smoothing her hands along the sides of her skirt.

The old strain resettled in the lines around her eyes.

"I'd better start supper," she said, slipping past him. Shortly I heard her opening cabinets and banging pots and pans around. Dad came and sat on the step where she had been. I tried to think of a way to leave without making matters worse.

"Neal, I'm very concerned," he said.

I waited, every muscle in my body tight.

"You've always been respectful and obedient. Up until recently I've never had any reason to worry about you."

I screwed up my face—I couldn't help it.

"What's the matter?" he asked. "Are you in pain?"

"No," I said. "You just make it sound as though I'd suddenly turned into a juvenile delinquent. I don't think I'm any worse than usual." To myself I added, And maybe I'm better.

"Your sister took this tack a while back, and you see where it's gotten *her*."

I chewed the inside of my cheek to keep from saying something that would send things downhill. I didn't know how to handle him. He couldn't listen to truth in any form without getting upset. We couldn't have a decent argument and come out better or closer on the other side of it. I could see his side of things better than he could ever see mine.

"This business about refusing to mow the churchyard, for example—"

I stood up abruptly. "Dad, I'm through with that! It's settled. Get off my case, and don't volunteer my services to anyone else without asking. I mean it!"

I was looking down at him, and for a moment he wavered—but only for a moment.

"Go to your room, and stay there until I tell you to come out!"

I almost laughed in his face. It was all I could do not to say, "Law', Br'er Sloan! *Please* don't throw me in the brier patch!" Instead I turned and went inside, moving fast through the kitchen before Mom could stop me.

In my room at last I locked the door and walked to the side window to look out, caught between giggling and yelling. It was so dumb! Did he think he could order us to our rooms forever when he felt himself losing control of us? Aileen and I could escape it one way or another, but then there was Georgie, the everlasting scapegoat. That was what kept me from doing something drastic—he'd catch all the anger meant for Aileen and me. It was serious business.

From where I stood I could see along the driveway between the Watkins' house and ours. Directly in my line of vision Aileen was getting out of Pete's car. She blew him a kiss and stood watching as he drove away. So she'd found him. I wondered how and where. The noise of the unmuffled engine burned the quiet air.

I slumped into the desk chair, waiting for the yelling to start down below. Then I heard the door to her room open and close softly. Ah! She'd gotten in unnoticed. I grinned in spite of myself. Who would've believed a week ago that I'd be rooting for Aileen? I opened the drawer and pulled out my battered music and a pencil.

Time passed quickly as I worked, building on the parts that were still legible on a few of the pages. I was surprised, then exhilarated as it came flooding back—the combinations of chords I'd worked out months ago were still in my head. I could feel them in my fingers, hear them in my head. The rumpled pages began to fill again. My pencil fairly flew. I hummed under my breath and drummed the rhythms on the desk edge. God, I wanted to play it!

A light tap on the door brought me back. In a panic I yanked open the drawer, then realized no one could get in until I unlocked the door. When the music was safely hidden, I closed the drawer carefully so that no telltale squeaks would give away my secret. I rumpled the bedcovers to make it look as though I'd been lying down, and then opened the door.

Mom was there with a tray of soup and sandwiches.

"Does this mean I have to stay up here till morning?" I asked, standing aside to let her in.

"He didn't say, I didn't ask. I just thought perhaps you'd rather eat up here." She set the tray down and turned to me. "I've been thinking, Neal—I suppose I wasn't taking some things into consideration when I told you to stop going to Jeanette's so much. It wasn't fair of me to make that kind of pronouncement. I want you to know that . . . I'll leave it to your good judgment."

I felt suddenly older and sadder. If only she'd said that in the beginning. "O.K. But you were probably right about my spending too much time there."

She took a breath as though she were about to say something else, but then she didn't. Instead she reached out and patted my arm. "Eat up. I'll get the tray later."

"Aileen might want something too," I said.

Mom's eyebrows went up. "She's home?"

"Yep. Has been for quite a while."

"Well, all right. I'll bring her something, and Georgie, too, when he wakes up from his nap. No need to disturb the peace."

"When can I come down?"

She cocked her head to one side. There was the ghost of mischief in her eyes. "I'm not going to services at the church tonight. I'm planning to be in bed with one of my headaches, so I won't know whether you come down or not."

I was grinning when I went back in my room to eat the soup and sandwiches. The mutiny was spreading.

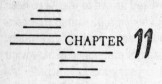

CHAPTER 11

By the time Dad drove away a little after seven, I'd already decided what I was going to do. I took the tray of empty dishes and went down to the kitchen to wash them. Then I went to the telephone and dialed Mrs. T.'s number.

"Hi," I said when she answered. "This is Neal."

"Well, so it is!" Her laughter was a bright, happy sound. "What's up?"

"A lot. Could I come over? I have Mom's permission."

"Of course you can come over! I've never said you couldn't. And you needn't go through all that business of ringing doorbells, either."

My spirits lifted. When I hung up, I went to Mom's room and tapped on the door. She was lying in bed, propped on two pillows, reading a novel.

"I washed my dishes," I announced, "and now I'm going to Mrs. T.'s for a little while. I've already called to see if it's O.K. with her."

She smiled. "Fine. Just don't stay too late. Your dad will be back around nine."

"Did he leave orders for me to stay in my room?"

"He never mentioned it again. In fact . . . well, he had other things on his mind, I suppose. He didn't seem to notice that none of you were around." Her frown deepened, and she pushed herself a little higher on the pillows.

"Good!" I said. "Maybe if we stay completely out of sight he'll forget we live here. That ought to cut down considerably on the conflict."

"Neal, be ashamed!" But she didn't sound as though she expected me to be sorry for the remark. "Go along—I'll see you when you get back."

The night was warm and damp. Clouds had moved in to cover the moon. I wondered vaguely how many times I'd crossed the street between our house and Mrs. T.'s during the past two years. I'd always taken for granted that I'd go on making the trek two or three times a day forever. Yet tonight it was a special privilege.

In spite of her invitation to walk right in, I turned the knob and opened the door cautiously, not as sure of my place now.

"Is that you, Neal?" she called from the kitchen. "Come on in! I'm making something special in honor of the occasion."

I shut the door behind me. "What occasion?"

She laughed. "Well, this is the first time you've been over today. It seems like several days, actually, since you were here. I miss having you around."

"Yeah," I said, coming into the kitchen where she was making some mountainous creation of ice cream and chocolate syrup. "I've missed being here."

"Well, it's good to have you back. You sounded mysterious over the telephone. I thought perhaps you'd told your folks about the music."

I shook my head "Not yet. Things aren't so good right now."

"Here, take your ice cream and we'll go sit in the other room. You can tell me about it."

We settled at the table by the large window. The smaller side windows were open. The wind had sprung up, sloshing waves against the shore below. Mrs. T.'s hair fell loosely to her shoulders. I noticed for the first time that its color was both blond and gray. The maroon caftan she wore made her look like a priestess or something. I studied her face, thinking how odd it was that she seemed to be no age at all. I couldn't tell if she was older or younger than Mom. How did you tell how old a person was, anyhow?

"Do I pass?" she asked gently.

"I'm sorry." I felt myself getting warm. "I didn't mean to stare."

"It's all right. I had the feeling you were looking at me for the first time."

"Maybe so. I've been doing that with everybody lately."

"Oh? Why?"

"We have a lot of trouble at our house. It's been there all along, but right now it seems like everything is getting worse. I don't know what to do."

She regarded me steadily. The dim light softened her face and hair until she seemed to blend into it, like a film not focused.

I struggled to explain. "See, people have the wrong idea about us. Maybe they think that because Dad is a minister we have it made when the knocks come. I don't know if they have visions of us kneeling around praying or what, but that's not the way it is. We don't talk about what bothers us. In fact, we're not supposed to *be* bothered with problems—we're above all that. I think Dad has swallowed that image of us hook, line, and sinker, but we're not fitting it."

I stopped, wondering if I was making any sense at all. She nodded. "Tell me about the trouble."

"It's hard to know where to begin. Everything is connected to everything else. I don't know . . ."

I felt that I was at the base of a huge mountain that grew even as I stood there watching, so that pretty soon I wouldn't be able to see the top of it or the end of it in either direction.

"Tell me one thing that has you worried."

"Georgie. I don't know whether he's sick in the head or I'm overdramatizing things. I've tried to picture myself telling someone else about how he is, and it always ends up with them patting me on the head and telling me that children his age have over-active imaginations and not to worry. Lately he's gotten pretty bad about telling things that aren't true, but he acts like he thinks they're true. He swears to them."

I tried to explain to her his idea that our real parents had been replaced by a False Mom and Dad, and his strange behavior. "I guess if I could be satisfied that he was only *thinking* it, I wouldn't feel so uneasy, but I have the feeling he's gone further than that."

"What do you mean?"

"I don't know." I got up from the table and began walking up and down the long room. "I just don't know. He decided this afternoon that I'm Real. He's not sure about Aileen. He thought she was False until Dad started treating her so—"

I stopped, realizing that I had gotten to a point where I'd have to decide how much to tell Mrs. T. After all, she was a member of Dad's congregation. Maybe it wasn't fair to burden her with all the mess going on at our house. What could she do about it?

"It's O.K.," she said, reading my mind. "Two heads are always better than one in a case like this. Maybe between us we can come up with a course of action. What about Aileen?"

I told her about Aileen's failure to graduate, and how Dad had yelled at her and made her stay in her room, about their long-standing war over everything under the sun and her ultimate weapon against him, Pete Cauthin.

"You know," I said, "I've thought up to now she was crazy, but I think I'm beginning to see more clearly why she's done it."

"Why?"

"To keep her sanity." I wandered over to the piano and touched the keys with one finger. "To stay real."

She got up and poured herself a cup of coffee. "Do you have any idea what's going on with your dad?"

"Some. Mom told me this afternoon—well, I'm not supposed to say this."

"You can trust me if you want to talk about it."

I let out my breath slowly. "I know that. God, I'm glad you're here!"

I went back to the table, but I didn't sit down. "He's thinking about leaving Gideon. I don't know why, exactly, unless he's realized it's now or never at his age. On the one hand, he hopes that people will keep on liking him for another few years so he can stay. On the other, it seems that he would like to make a new beginning somewhere else."

"That's a scary decision to make," she commented. "I know what it feels like. I had to give up my home and some dear friends when I left Chicago to come to North Carolina. I was terribly afraid."

That surprised me. I've never thought of Mrs. T. being afraid—she always seems so sure of herself.

"Then why . . . how could you do it?"

"I had to face up to the fact that I wasn't happy there. I needed to get away from some . . . negative influences. It was a good choice. I'm not sorry I made it, but at the same time it was certainly scary."

I nodded. "I can understand that—Dad's probably scared, too. But I still wish he'd leave. People here seem to like him and he does everything to please them, but he's not happy about it. If he was, he wouldn't be so hard to live with!"

"Do you think he likes being a minister?"

I made a face. "I think he likes the attention it gets him. He likes to perform. Maybe he should have gone on the stage."

Mrs. T. laughed. "Neal, you're such a cynic!"

"You would be, too, if you could see him the way I do. The thing is, he can't get the rest of us in the family to 'do right.' I think he's convinced *we'll* lose his job for him."

She leaned both elbows on the table and propped her chin in her hands. Her eyes looked beyond me, beyond the room, beyond Gideon. Three deep lines creased her forehead above the bridge of her nose. After a while she said, "What are you most afraid of?"

It wasn't a psychology question—she asked as though she wanted a real answer, to fit into a puzzle she was trying to put together.

"I guess . . . I'm afraid we will all come apart at the seams. In fact, it feels as though we've begun unraveling already, and it's happening faster and faster." I was beginning to feel hopeless. "Dad would never admit that we have problems and need help. Mom for some reason is afraid to stand up to him. Georgie is too little. Aileen's way doesn't get her anything but grief. And I—"

"Yes?"

I hit the table with my fist. "It isn't fair! Why do I have to be the one to do something? I had it all figured out, how to stay out of the line of fire. How not to cause trouble. How not to call attention to myself. Now all of a sudden I seem to be doing *all* those things, whether I want to or not! Why?"

She shrugged. "Maybe because you're basically honest. Maybe because you can't stand to see people you care about being hurt. Maybe because you aren't selfish. Those are all good reasons."

"Mrs. T., I can't take it. I'm not like Aileen—I don't enjoy conflict. I don't like stabbing people or rubbing them raw with words. In my experience fighting doesn't get you anywhere but in trouble."

I thought about the struggle with Pete in his boat. What was the good of it? I'd lost my temper, and now he was my sworn enemy. If I'd been able to hold my tongue five minutes longer—

She went to the piano and sat down. "You said your mother told you it was all right to come over whenever you liked now."

It was a statement. but I knew the question that it implied. "She had second thoughts. Maybe after having me around full time, she wasn't so sure she wanted to handle me all by herself."

She laughed, but then she became serious again. "You still aren't telling about the music, though."

I shook my head. "No—but don't worry about it. I've already figured out how I can practice at the church. I won't put you on the spot. I realize now that it hasn't been fair to you to make you keep my secret."

"Now that I know more about what's been going on at your house, *I'm* having second thoughts," she said.

"It's funny. I was really mad at you yesterday for turning me out. That's what it felt like. I felt like a pet kitten that's been coddled and looked after inside a warm house and then all of a sudden has to fend for himself in the great, cold outdoors."

"You don't feel that way still?"

"No." I was surprised at my own answer. "I still need your help with the music. No one else around here can do that for me. But I've leaned on you too much for everything else as well, practically living over here to keep from living *there*. That's not too mature."

She smiled again and began playing chords on the piano. "What would you like to hear?"

I moved my chair closer, where I could watch her fingers move over the keys. "Anything. Anything at all."

For maybe half an hour I just sat and listened. It was better than church. In fact, this is what church ought to be like, filling me up with peace and beauty and making me feel strong again.

"It's after nine, and tomorrow's a school day," she said, when the final chord died away.

I started up. I'd meant to be home before Dad got back from church.

"Thanks, Mrs. T.," I said at the door. Then I did something I had never done before. I leaned over and kissed her on the cheek. "I sure am glad you're alive!"

And I left in a hurry, before I could see how she felt about that.

CHAPTER 12

The long talk with Mrs. T. helped me, in the days that followed, to ease up on Dad some—and on Mom, too, since she had to deal with his moods more directly than the rest of us did He still wasn't easy to live with, but luckily nothing like the mowing job came up to make us clash head-on.

Aileen was very cool toward me. We didn't argue, but I guess she thought she had to choose between Pete and me, because of the fight. Naturally, she chose Pete. I made a point of avoiding him at school—no easy task, believe me! I lurked behind many a classroom door just staying out of his sight.

Georgie's secretive look and his silent appearing and disappearing were more apparent to me now that I knew his theory about the False Family. He wouldn't talk about it, though, in spite of the fact that our afternoon on Captain's boat had made us allies. Of course, if he wasn't going to bring it up, *I* certainly didn't intend to. Maybe if enough time passed he would outgrow the notion. Still, I intended to do whatever I could to assure him that I, at least, was r

"You want to walk with me to school?" I asked him at breakfast one morning. I gulped down the rest of my milk, waiting for him to answer.

He gave me that quick, testing look. "Maybe. If I'm ready when you leave."

Frankly, I was surprised at his lack of enthusiasm. I thought he'd be glad for my company.

Fifteen minutes later when I was ready to go, he was still fussing around in his room. "You'll be late," I said.

"I have to find my reading book," he said stubbornly. "You go ahead."

"I'll help you look for it." I started examining the neat piles of books on his desk.

"You don't have to do that."

"What've you got in your book bag?" I asked. "Maybe you already put your reading book in it." I reached over and unbuckled the book bag lying on his bed. Sure enough, there lay the reading book and some arithmetic papers, all ready to go. With them was a can of soup and a huge candy bar.

"Oh," he said, not looking me in the eye. "I must've put it in there last night."

"For Pete's sake, Georgie! What're you doing with a whole can of soup in there? You can't eat that for lunch."

"I'm taking it to . . . somebody," he said.

"The candy bar, too? Mom wouldn't like it if she knew."

"It's my stuff!" he said, his voice rising. "You shouldn't bother my stuff!"

My mind did an instant replay of the moment days ago when Pete Cauthin's hand had probed the knapsack full of music books, and how I'd felt. I was ashamed.

"Oh, come on." I rebuckled the bag. "Let's go. I won't tell Mom."

The day was cloudy, threatening rain. Georgie walked beside me quietly, responding with monosyllables to anything I said. When we neared the corner of Salton and Water streets, he began skipping ahead.

"Be careful, Georgie—look both ways!" I called after him.

He looked both ways obediently, then skipped across the street.

"O.K., wait up!" I quickened my pace, but he just grinned at me and started running. The distance between us widened, and then suddenly he was no longer there. I blinked and looked again, sure that my eyes were playing tricks—I'd been watching him the whole time. I ran to the spot where I'd seen him last, but there was no sign of him.

"This is dumb!" I said aloud. I was directly in front of the Tayntons' house, where there is nothing to hide behind. The yard is flat and there are no hedges—just a border of irises along the walkway and a few scraggly bushes up against the house.

"Georgie, quit playing now and come on!" I didn't want to yell too loudly. The Tayntons might still be in bed at this time of morning.

The front door opened, and old Mrs. Taynton came shuffling out on the porch in housecoat and slippers. Her hair was mashed under a net. She smiled when she recognized me.

"Heyo, Neal! What's the trouble?"

"I'm sorry if I bothered you," I said. "My brother was walking to school with me. He ran on ahead and then—disappeared, right in front of your house. I thought he might be hiding."

"I wouldn't worry about it if I was you," she said. "He's teasin'. You go along to school and you'll see he'll come arunnin' when he knows you aren't goin' to take the time to look for him. You stay here lookin' and you'll be late yourself."

"Well . . . maybe you're right. Thanks." I started away, still uneasy. I kept looking back over my shoulder until I rounded the corner and went up Salton Street, the way we usually go.

I tore into homeroom about five minutes before the bell rang and threw my books on the desk. "Ms. Garfield, I have to go over to the elementary building to talk to my little brother's teacher!"

"Is something wrong, Neal?"

"I'm not sure he got to school this morning," I said. "I have to find out."

She gave me a puzzled look, but let me go. I ran all the way over to the elementary building. The bell was ringing just as I got to the door of his classroom, and Miss Harvey was standing there ushering the Munchkins inside.

"Miss Harvey, Georgie—" I began, all out of breath, and then

I looked past her into the room. He was in his seat, coloring something with a red crayon.

"What about Georgie, Neal?"

"How long has he been here?"

"Oh—about three minutes, I suppose."

I was really burned up. "May I speak with him out here, please?"

"Well, of course." She turned and called Georgie. When he looked up and saw me standing there, all sorts of expressions chased across his face.

"Neal wants to talk to you, Georgie."

He got up and came as far as the door, but he wouldn't come all the way out of the room. Miss Harvey sort of pushed him in my direction, but he resisted.

"What's the matter, Georgie?" she asked, looking from him to me.

He wouldn't answer. "We were walking to school together, and he ran off and left me," I said.

He looked down at his feet.

"Georgie, did you do that?" Miss Harvey squatted down beside him and put her arm around him. "Why'd you run away?"

He looked at her and didn't blink. "I didn't," he said in the flat voice he uses when he's lying. "He was walking too slow. I was afraid I'd be late. He just didn't keep up."

"Georgie, that's a bald-faced lie! You *know* you ran, and when I called you to wait, you ran all the harder!"

I could tell Miss Harvey didn't know which one to believe. I straightened. "Well, at least he got here all right. I was worried about him. It's O.K. I'm sorry I blew my top."

"You may go back to your seat, Georgie," Miss Harvey said. "But is there anything you'd like to say to Neal before he leaves?"

"No, ma'am." His eyes were on the floor again.

"Are you sure?"

"Yes, ma'am."

He went back into the room, and Miss Harvey stepped outside

and closed the door behind her. "Neal, you might tell your mother that I think she and I should have a conference pretty soon."

"Is he doing poor work?"

"N-no, not exactly. He just seems preoccupied. I thought perhaps—"

"I'll tell her," I said. "I have to go to class now." I walked away as fast as I could, before I ended up telling her that Georgie had plenty to be preoccupied about.

Homeroom was over and the bell was ringing for first period class when I got back to the high school building. I plowed through the crowd coming out of the room so I could get my books and make it to the end of the hall before next bell. I felt like a salmon heading upstream.

It isn't smart to be in too much of a hurry. Out in the hall again I didn't watch where I was going, and the next thing I knew I'd run smack into someone coming from the other direction. Books, papers, and pencils flew everywhere and were immediately trampled by dozens of feet. I bumped against a locker and for a couple of seconds didn't know which end was up.

"You did that on purpose, you nut!" The bellowing voice belonged to none other than Pete Cauthin. He loomed in front of me, his hands already balled into fists. I despaired at my rotten luck. Of all people in the whole damn school!

"Sorry, Pete!" I mumbled, scrambling for everything that had dropped, his and mine. "I wasn't looking—"

"Oh, fine! Knock all my stuff from here to East Jesus and all you can say is 'Sorry, Pete!' One more—"

"Here." I shoved books and notebooks into his arms. "It's all there. I got to go."

I barely made it to English class, only to discover when the time came to hand in my homework assignment that my paper wasn't there. I knew I'd had it when I left home. It must have gotten lost in the scuffle in the hall.

I raised my hand. "Mr. Hampton?"

Mr. Hampton is a good-looking bearded guy in his thirties. All the girls get crushes on him, but he is strictly no-nonsense.

"What is it, Neal?"

"My paper. I think it's on the floor in the hall."

He frowned. "That's the first time I've ever heard *that* excuse."

"My books got knocked out of my hands. I thought I'd picked everything up, but I don't have the paper."

"All right—you may go look for it. Be back in five minutes."

The hall was empty. I walked the full length of it, up one side and down the other. No sign of the paper.

When I got back to the room, Mr. Hampton was well along with the day's lesson. He finished the lecture, made a class writing assignment, then called me to his desk.

"You didn't find the paper?"

"No, sir."

"Do you have any idea where it might be?"

"Yes, sir, I do. But it might as well be at the bottom of the river. Would you let me do the assignment over? I have the rough draft at home. I don't think I'll get the paper back."

Mr. Hampton sighed a little. "Well, all right. What was your topic?"

"I wrote about a guy named Thelonious Monk."

His eyes seemed to sharpen. "Oh? I didn't know you were interested in jazz." I thought his voice was unnecessarily loud, and I guess I was amazed he recognized the name.

"Well, I just had a book with some stuff in it that looked interesting." I tried to sound offhand. "Writing the paper was a way to learn something new."

"Go ahead and do the class assignment for now," he said. "I'll give you an extra two days to rewrite the paper."

Other than that, it was an ordinary kind of school day. But then shortly before the final bell at the end of last period, the intercom came on in math class and I was asked to report to the principal's office. Mrs. Ricks sent me down without asking any questions, which was a good thing. I was just as mystified as she was.

A few minutes later Pete Cauthin, Mr. Hampton, and I were crowded into Mr. Thompson's inner office. Pete looked sullen and angry, Mr. Hampton cold.

Mr. Thompson is on the beefy side—probably played football in his younger days. He smoothed his hair over his bald spot. His chair squeaked as he swung it from side to side, looking us over.

"Well, Pete, it has been three days since I talked to you," he said. "Where've you been so long?"

I didn't think it was so smart for him to be sarcastic. Since Pete couldn't beat up Mr. Thompson without dire consequences, he was likely to take out his anger later on a more likely victim—me. Pete wouldn't answer the question.

"All right, Mr. Hampton. What's this all about?" Mr. Thompson asked.

Mr. Hampton handed Mr. Thompson some papers. "This is a report that Pete handed in to me fifth period as part of a homework assignment I'd given. I have reason to believe it isn't his work—that he copied someone else's paper and claimed it for his own."

I began to feel slightly sick. I watched Mr. Thompson take the papers and glance over the first page.

"Thelonious Sphere Monk: Jazz Innovator," he read aloud. "Hmmm. Well, Pete, I must say it surprises me that you would pick such a topic to write a report on." He tossed the papers on the desk. "Is that your handwriting?"

"Yes," he mumbled.

"Do you concur that it is his handwriting, Mr. Hampton?"

"Yes, I do."

"What makes you think it isn't his work?"

"Neal Sloan is in my first period English class," Mr. Hampton said. At his words I suddenly seemed to become visible to Mr. Thompson. "He had the same assignment as Pete did—I had given it to all my classes. This morning he didn't hand in the paper, which he said he had done but couldn't find. He told me that he had written his report on Monk, that he thought he knew where the paper might be, but that he didn't think he could get it back. He asked for permission to do the assignment over, which I granted."

"I see," said Mr. Thompson, eyeing me. I tried to keep my face expressionless. I didn't look at Pete. "And did Neal suggest that Pete had taken the paper?"

"No, he didn't. He made no accusations. If Pete hadn't handed this in, I would never have known."

Mr. Thompson swung his chair slightly. "Well, Pete, what do you have to say for yourself?"

Pete's face was blotched with patches of pink. "I handed in my paper, like I was supposed to. I don't know why Mr. Hampton thinks it was me stole Neal's paper 'stead of the other way around. Except his daddy's a preacher and Neal's such a goody-goody nobody ever thinks he does anything wrong—"

Mr. Thompson held up a hand. "That's enough, Pete. I asked you what you had to say for yourself, not against Neal. I'll be more direct: did you do the reading and research for the paper you handed in today?"

Pete hesitated a moment. "Yes," he said finally.

Mr. Thompson turned to me. "Neal, would you look at these papers and tell me whether they contain the material you used for your report?"

I took the pages and looked through them. As far as I could tell, it was word for word what I had written, except it was in Pete's scrawl. I put them back on the desk.

"Yes," I said. "That's mine."

"Still going to stick to your story, Pete?"

"Sure!"

"All right then—I'm going to play Solomon. Each of you is going to have a chance to tell me all you know about Thelonious Monk. Pete, you're first."

He knew then that he was caught, but for some reason he was too stubborn to admit it. "Well . . . ah . . . he was born in . ah Rocky Mount, North Carolina. See, he's a native of our own state. And . . ah . . . he was a far-out piano player."

He stopped. We waited.

"That's all you remember? Looks like you would've learned more than that even copying the paper."

Pete glared at Mr. Thompson. For about three seconds I thought he might leap over the desk and strangle the man.

Thompson turned to me. "O.K., Neal, what can *you* tell us about Monk?"

In a low voice I told a few facts, thinking all the time that, either way, I'd lose. I was aware of Mr. Thompson's thoughtful look as he listened, as though he were seeing me for the first time. When I had finished, Mr. Thompson nodded, picked up the papers, and returned them to Mr. Hampton.

"I believe you can treat this as Neal's paper, all right. Pete, you wait in the outside office while I speak with Neal."

"Rat!" Pete muttered as he went out. I kept my mouth shut.

"Mr. Hampton and I would like to clarify a few things," Mr. Thompson said. "Tell us how Pete got your paper without your knowing about it."

"Well, it was sort of a fluke." I told them about the collision in the hall. "It was my fault—I wasn't looking where I was going—but I picked up all the stuff both of us had dropped. I suppose my paper got in with his things."

"Why didn't you go directly to him and ask for the paper as soon as you discovered it was missing?"

I could feel my face getting warm. "Well, I guess you could say we've had a falling-out."

"I see." He tapped on his desk with a pencil. "Well, I'm warning you—don't start any fights here in school, understand?"

He ought to know I'd be about the last guy in school to start a fight. "Yes, sir."

"All right—you may go. And send in Pete on your way out."

I left the office, my shirt clinging to my body. "He's ready for you," I said to Pete, motioning with my thumb.

He didn't say anything, just gave me a dirty look as he brushed by me. I knew I was a marked man.

CHAPTER 13

Making my way across the school grounds that afternoon, I pondered mathematical probabilities—the number of chances in a million that I'd collide with Pete Cauthin in the school hall. It seemed an incredible piece of bad luck. It would've been better to knock down Mr. Thompson himself. At least he would believe in the accidental nature of things. Pete never would. Thank goodness school would be over in a few weeks, but now, more than ever, I had to stay out of his way. It wouldn't be easy.

I felt like a tightrope walker strung between two enemies—trouble at school, trouble at home. Where was a guy supposed to go to get away? I looked at my watch. Too early to go to Mrs. T.'s—she had her regular students afternoons after school. I longed for an empty room with a piano as a thirsty person must long for cold water. When I turned the corner at Salton Street, I knew my only option for now was the piano in the sanctuary of Gideon Baptist Church.

Set back from the corner, it looked vacant and useless as only a church can on a Monday afternoon, but I was glad for the emptiness. Fortunately, when a bunch of Baptists get through with Sunday, it takes them about two days to rest up. I could probably count on all the time I wanted there if I didn't turn on any lights to attract attention. Lately I'd been going there only at the dinner hour, but right now I was feeling desperate.

Just thinking ahead to the moment when I'd be at a keyboard again made me walk faster. I'd go home to get my key and music books and be back in fifteen minutes. Everybody and everything else could go hang as far as I was concerned—the rest of the afternoon was going to be mine.

There are three entrances to the church, all of which are supposed to be locked when the building's not in use. Until a couple of years ago the place was never locked, but then when the communion silver was stolen, the deacons decided that only certain people should have keys.

I'm not one of them. You wouldn't believe the trouble I went to two years ago in order to have a key of my own. I borrowed the one I needed from Dad's key ring, caught the nine-thirty bus to Wayside, got the key duplicated, and caught the five-thirty bus back to Gideon. I was thirteen at the time, and in a sweat the whole day for fear Dad would notice the key was missing, but since he rarely uses the back door, he never found out.

The key hangs on a nail behind the clothes in my closet, along with some others that don't open any doors that I know about. So far as Mom knows, they're all junk keys.

She was talking on the telephone when I came in, a stroke of good luck to balance the run of bad luck I've been having. I ran upstairs, grabbed my music from the desk drawer, took the key from the closet nail, and ran down again. Mom was still on the phone. I heard her say into the phone, "Just a minute," and then, "Neal, where are you going in such a hurry?"

"Something I have to tend to. Back in a little while!" I was already out the door headed up the street before she could say anything else. I'd think up a plausible answer to give when I came back, but right now I was in too much of a hurry to bother.

The rear entrance of the church is hidden from the street by a cluster of cedar trees someone planted as a windbreak years ago. I went to the corner, walked up Salton Street until I was pretty sure I was out of Miss Patterson's line of vision, checked all around to be certain no one was looking, and then ambled in the direction of the cemetery. Three minutes later I was inside the church, breathing the stuffy air of the back hallway. After I locked the door behind me, I stood for a moment listening. Hearing nothing but the usual pops and creaks of old wood settling, I went into the sanctuary.

The afternoon light filtering through the purple panes gave the place a jukebox glow. I sat down at the piano and opened the lid. The yellowed keys grinned up at me like the teeth of an ancient skeleton. Here and there a missing ivory left a gray gap. I brushed my hands over the keys, feeling their unevenness. The man who tunes it told Miss Phifer once that it had a better tone than most of the new uprights, and that if it was kept free of mice and moths there was no need to invest in a new one if we didn't mind the looks of this one.

Of course, Mr. Mac was glad about *that*, not being one to spend money unnecessarily, either his or the church's. Besides, he donated the piano in the first place.

I set my books on the rack and began practicing scales and finger exercises, gingerly at first because the sound seemed so loud in the emptiness. Gradually, though, I forgot everything else. It felt so good. Everything else about my life seemed far away— only the music was real.

After the exercises came the improvising, my favorite thing. So much of it is done in my head away from a piano that I have to test it to see if it translates into the right sounds on the instrument. I'm still not that good, but Mrs. T. seems pleased that I manage as well as I do, considering I've never heard a live performance except on TV. At one time or another I've listened to every recording she has, and I've learned the styles of Thelonious Monk and Bud Powell, Erroll Garner and Chick Corea, and others too. She says the idea is to learn everything you can from them, but not to imitate.

"Neal," she told me once, "you have a real genius for jazz. I don't understand it, considering that you haven't been exposed to it here in Gideon, but you're a natural. Just think—suppose I'd played Beethoven or Mozart the day you came over to fill my woodbox?"

"I probably would've yawned and gone home," I said.

But maybe that isn't true. I like Beethoven and Mozart O.K.—it's just that they seem already set in stone—you play them more or less the way they are, the way the marks on the page tell you to play them. But jazz is different. It grows and changes all the time in your mind and under your fingers. Nobody plays any piece the same way another person does.

I worked on one number, playing it over and over, filling in and changing as I went along. It sounded good to me—full, rich rhythm in the bass, bright, dissonant chords and rapid, running notes in the treble. I was completely wrapped up in what I was doing when I heard the definite click of a door latch closing.

I spun on the wobbly round piano stool. Mr. Mac stood at the back of the church, staring at me, one hand on the brass doorknob, the other hanging limply by his side.

"Hello, Mr. Mac," I said. My voice was dry and thin in the still air.

"I never knew you could play the piano," he said. He walked down the aisle toward me, looking interested. He was like a dream person whose behavior is pleasant enough, but I had the feeling that if I said any of the wrong things he'd turn into a monster before my very eyes.

"Well, I can't really," I began, hearing the feeble words for what they were—a lie. I wondered how long he'd been there listening. "I just sort of like to come in every now and then and fool around with it."

I turned on the stool and began gathering notes and books. My hands shook.

"I reckon you have permission to do this," he said, coming over to stand by the piano. He leaned against it, having to lift his right elbow to rest it on the top.

"No, I haven't."

I closed the piano lid and waited, wondering if I'd ever be able to swallow again. I couldn't think. It was purely a matter of blind defense now. I was too scared to anticipate, to make up answers before the questions could be asked.

"How did you get in?"

"I have a key."

The ghost of a frown settled briefly on his brow and then disappeared. "Well, I guess it's all right. Thing is, if you use the lights, or turn on the heat in winter—"

I shook my head. "I don't do either. I'm not here that often, really." If he was mainly worried about the church paying a higher utility bill on my account, I wanted to reassure him.

"Sounds to me like you're pretty good on that thing," he went on, switching directions. His bent index finger tapped on the piano lid lightly. I could feel his searching eyes. Surely he could see that I was shaking!

"Naw—I think it's kind of interesting." I got up, holding the books low by my left side, thankful I hadn't brought more of them this time.

"Can you read music?"

"A little. I've sort of taught myself."

"I think it's a good thing to know. My old daddy made us all take lessons right here on this very instrument." Mr. Mac chuckled suddenly. "A teacher came to the house and gave one lesson after another to me and my brother and our three sisters. That poor woman sure earned her pay!"

I tried to smile, although I didn't feel like it.

"Maybe you ought to take lessons," he said.

I shook my head. "I really don't want to—don't have time." Saying the words made me feel sick inside, like I had betrayed a friend.

He wouldn't let it die. "We could use another pianist in this church. Lola Phifer won't be here forever."

"Well, she'll be here longer than I will." I ducked my head slightly. "I expect I'd better be going. Mom will have dinner about ready."

"I'm going too," he said. "You come in the front door?"

"No, sir The back."

"You got a key to the back?"

"I . . . borrowed Dad's." Well, it was true I'd borrowed it two years ago to have my own made.

Mr. Mac studied me for another few moments. "Well, just be sure you lock up after yourself as you leave. Don't want the communion silver taken again!"

"Yes, sir. I will." I could feel his eyes still upon me as I left the sanctuary and went down the dark little hall to the back door.

Outside again, I locked the door and tried the knob just to be sure. As I turned to go down the steps, the significance of what had just happened hit me. My knees gave way, and I sat down, overwhelmed by the kind of feeling I've known only in the worst nightmares. This was what I had dreaded most, but now I realized I hadn't expected it. Somehow, not being discovered in two years had made me believe it would never happen. How could I have been so stupid? Why had I never planned what I'd do and say if I got caught?

Much later I got up from the steps and walked into the cemetery. I don't know how long I wandered up and down the even rows, reading names but not really seeing them, trying to think. Most of the gravestones in the old part of the cemetery lean slightly, as though the dirt holding them up has lost its muscle. I didn't want to be dead, but I couldn't help thinking that at least these folks didn't have to worry any more about fear or shame. There's something to be said for that.

I couldn't count on Mr. Mac's keeping his mouth shut—it was about as likely as the chances for snow in Miami. Briefly I considered going after him and asking him not to tell, but he would want to know why. Pretty soon it would be all over Gideon. My folks would be angry at me for keeping it a secret from them. Worse, they'd be angry at Mrs. T. for helping me keep it a secret.

I left the graveyard and walked through all the backyards on the street to our house, still not knowing as I opened the back screen door what I was going to do. I guess I hoped for a flash of light and a voice out of the sky.

"Well, I was about to send out a posse," Mom said when I walked into the kitchen. "Dinner will be ready soon."

"O.K.," I mumbled, not stopping. I held the books close to my side.

"Where have you been?"

"Up the street," I said, already halfway down the hall. I raced up to my room and stuffed the books in my desk drawer. In the mirror over the chest of drawers a pale, desperate-looking face stared dumbly back at me.

"Think, goddammit!" I growled at the reflection and watched it mouth the words like some ventriloquist's dummy.

You pitiful jackass! What're you going to do now—go down and confess your secret life before Mr. Mac beats you to it?

The pale face seemed to plead with me not to expect too much.

"You dumb ass!" I hissed at it.

"Who?"

I jerked around. Aileen was leaning against the door jamb.

"Why don't you knock once in a while?" I snapped.

"I do, once in a while. But the door was open so there wasn't anything to knock on."

"Well, what do you want? Or do you just spy on people in your spare time?"

"I wasn't spying. I wasn't here two seconds before I spoke. Who's a dumb ass?"

"None of your business. Beat it!"

"You sure are hard to get along with all of a sudden."

"Look, I don't like people hanging around my door staring at me. How'd you feel if I did that to you?"

"Not too good, I suppose." She came all the way into the room and sat on my bed.

"You have a hearing problem, don't you?" I pointed to my mouth. "Here—read my lips. *Get out!*"

"Sh!" She held a finger to her lips. "Better shut the door before

Mom comes up to see what all the yelling's about."

I glared at her, but I shut the door anyway.

"This touchiness wouldn't have anything to do with your visit to Mr. Thompson's office today, would it?"

"How'd you know about that? Aw, forget it—I should've known Pete would tell you."

She studied me. I waited for her to tell me what a twerp I was. "Pete says you got him in trouble," she said finally.

"I didn't get him in trouble! If he's in trouble it's his own fault—he expected me to cover for him when he cheated!"

"Tell me about it."

"You probably won't believe me if I do. I bumped into him in the hall because I was late to class and wasn't watching where I was going. It was an accident. God knows I'd never deliberately ram him! Our books and stuff got scattered, and when I picked it all up and gave him back what I thought was his, I gave him my English paper by mistake."

I told her how I'd gone back to search for it later and when I didn't find it, had gotten permission from Mr. Hampton to re-write. "I never told Hampton that Pete had my paper. He asked me my topic and I told him. Later on, Pete handed in my paper, which he'd copied over in his own handwriting. Hampton nailed him. We had court in the office to prove who the paper belonged to. That's it. I never accused him. It was dumb for him to think he wouldn't get caught!"

My voice had gotten louder and louder. The last words hit the air and bounced back at me. *Caught caught caught*, like a crow call, mocking.

"I believe you," she said simply.

"Thanks. Now if you don't mind, I'd like to have a little privacy."

She got up obligingly and started toward the door. "Neal, something's the matter, isn't it?"

"No," I lied. "Everything is just fine! Now leave—"

And let me get calmed down so when the firing squad lines up in front of me, I'll be cool. Through my window I could see a patch of blue sky bisected by the Watkins' pitched roof. It was like a view from a prison window.

The door shut softly behind her. I closed my eyes and breathed deeply to try to loosen the tightness in my chest. How to explain this terrible, peculiar fear? It's like when the hotshot champion basketball team of the world is about to lose, and you're on their side and know that nothing will bail them out. Or it's like when two cars are heading straight for each other and there's no time to warn the drivers. How much time did I have? I kept replaying the afternoon. If only I'd waited another hour to go to the church, I might have missed Mr. Mac. It's what I got for being impatient and throwing caution to the winds.

Maybe he didn't hear much of what I was playing. Maybe it just sounded like banging to him and he wouldn't give it a second thought. But then, he might start teasing me in front of everyone next Sunday—

God! I flung myself face first on the bed and covered my head with the pillow. If I could be a thousand miles from here!

"Neal! Come to dinner!" I barely heard Mom through the pillow, but there was no mistaking the annoyance in her voice. She'd probably called me several times already. I jumped up and grabbed a comb.

"Coming!" I hollered. A quick trip to the bathroom to throw cold water on my face and I hurried downstairs. When I came into the dining room, the other members of the family were waiting, Dad harried-looking and short-tempered, Mom tired. Georgie's face was blank as a mask—maybe he was determined to hide from me after running away this morning. Aileen, on the other hand, looked as though she could read minds, and would, if necessary. I pulled out my chair and sat, dreading the reprimands that would follow.

"Well, at last we can have dinner," said Dad. "Aileen, will you say grace?"

I stared. There's no remembering when any of us besides Dad

has said grace at table. For a minute I thought Aileen was going to lose her cool, but she didn't. She swallowed hard as we all bowed our heads. Then out of her mouth came the rote blessing that Dad has said all these years, only she said it carefully, picking her way through the unfamiliar territory of old words. It was kind of nice. After she said, "Amen," Georgie raised his head and looked at her through his thick glasses, his face pinched with concentration. Even when Mom began passing the food, he didn't take his eyes off Aileen. I figured he was about to decide she was Real, after all.

I glanced around furtively, trying to gauge the mood. Some crazy part of me wanted to blurt: *Look, you guys, I've been taking piano lessons from Mrs. Talbot for two years! I want to be a jazz pianist. . . .*

I could imagine four pairs of eyes swiveling toward me, amazed and full of questions. Why did I choose now to make the announcement? Why all the secrecy? How'd I manage? How did I pay for the lessons? Jazz? You mean . . . *jazz?*

When the telephone rang, I must've jumped a mile.

"I'll get it!" I said. My hand hit the iced tea glass beside my plate and knocked it over, spreading a brown stain across the table.

"For Heaven's sake, Neal!" Mom was exasperated. The telephone rang again. "Just get a cloth and wipe up the mess you've made. *I'll* get the phone."

I raced to the kitchen, grabbed a dish towel, and raced back. For a person who didn't want to call attention to himself I wasn't doing so well. I could feel Aileen's eyes probing as I mopped the puddle of tea.

Mom came back and sat down. "It was Ava Patterson. I told her we were eating."

Not Mr. Mac, thank goodness. Relief. Then I had a sudden thought—could Miss Patterson have seen me going into the church, after all?

"Who did she want to speak to?" I asked.

"Your father, of course." Mom gave me a curious look, and I realized the question sounded ridiculous coming from me.

"I'm sorry about spilling the tea," I said, partly in apology, partly to divert attention.

"It's all right," she said.

"You're acting very jumpy," Dad commented. "One would think you expected that call to be for you—or *about* you."

The silence that followed his words seemed hours long. When I finally spoke, my throat felt dry. "Nope. I was just trying to be helpful for a change. Every time we sit down to eat, the telephone rings, and Mom always has to get up to answer it."

Her surprised, grateful look made me feel more miserable than ever. I don't even know where that excuse came from. I took the sopping dish towel back to the kitchen and spent more time than was necessary rinsing it.

"Neal!" Dad called. "Are you coming back to the table or not?"

"Yes, sir. I'm coming."

Play it by ear, I cautioned myself as I sat down at my place again. Wait for the right moment. Don't start something before you have to.

The word "propitious" popped into my head. Mr. Hampton made us learn five new vocabulary words a week, and that was on last week's list. It's not a word a person can work into a conversation in Gideon, North Carolina. Mr. Hampton had explained that it meant fortunate or favorable. I remembered it because the example he gave was how in surfing a person has to figure the wave just right in order to ride it in all the way. A moment too early or too late and he gets smashed.

The problem is you have to know so damned much about waves to recognize the propitious moment.

CHAPTER 14

Aileen paid a lot of attention to Georgie, offering to serve his plate and asking him direct questions. It was the way she had been in the old days, when he was little and she was sort of his second mother. He began to warm to it in spite of himself, flashing her a grateful glance now and then. He wouldn't talk much, though. Maybe he was afraid if he made too much of it she'd go away again.

As meals at our house go, this one was fairly peaceful. If I hadn't been so strung out, I might have enjoyed it, but my mind kept replaying the picture of Mr. Mac coming down the church aisle toward me. I made myself eat the food on my plate even though I had no appetite—I didn't want any unnecessary questions. Afterward Aileen took over Georgie's evening ritual, helping with his bath, promising a bedtime story. Dad withdrew to his study, leaving me to help Mom with the cleanup. We cleared the table in silence, taking things into the kitchen, dodging and crisscrossing each other's path like dancers.

"I had a long talk with Miss Harvey on the telephone this afternoon," she said suddenly. I was drying the dishes, and my mind was not in this place. It took me a couple of seconds to realize who she was talking about.

"Georgie's teacher? Yeah—I meant to tell you she wanted to have a conference."

"What's this about Georgie running away this morning?"

So much had happened since then that I had shoved the incident to the back of my mind. Now the strangeness of it came back with full force. I told her how he had seemed to vanish into thin air and then reappear at his desk at school.

"It was like something out of *Star Trek*—you know, like he was beamed up."

"That's strange. He likes being with you so much. Why do you think he'd run from you?"

I was silent, wondering what to tell. The candy bar and the can of soup in his book bag were a part of the mystery. "I'm not sure. Did you ask him?"

"No, I wanted to get the story from you before I confronted him with it. Miss Harvey is worried. She thinks he's . . . losing touch with reality."

Fear shot through me. It was one thing to entertain the notion myself, but for someone outside the family to say it put a different light on things.

"I . . . think she may be right. Georgie's not like other kids, Mom." Even as I said the words I felt a sense of doom.

She took her hands out of the dishwater, dried them, poured herself a glass of tea, and sat down at the kitchen table. I'd never seen her do that before. Mom's a stickler for finishing what she starts before she gives herself any time off.

"That day Georgie and I went to Wayside, I went to Dr. Koch," she said rapidly, as though if she didn't make it quick her tongue would lock, "to see whether he could recommend some help."

"For Georgie? That's great, Mom—he needs help, and he needs it soon. What did Dr. Koch say?"

"There's a psychiatric clinic in Hatboro. It's pretty expensive, and we'd have to make the trip at least once a week for . . . as long as necessary. The thing is—"

She stopped and took a swallow of tea. "The thing is, Dr. Koch says that Georgie's problems may not be his alone. Before it's over others in the family may be in counseling too."

The full significance of what she was saying pressed down on us. "What does Dad say?" I asked.

She clamped her fingers into a fist, like someone who has a sudden, sharp pain. "I haven't told him yet. I'm going to."

"He'll blow his top," I said. "What're you going to do then?"

She was like an animal caught by the leg, struggling to escape. I felt sorry for her, but I felt sorrier for Georgie.

"I don't know. The counseling sessions will cost a good bit. Our health insurance will take care of some of it, but I have no money of my own. . . ."

I stared. "Doesn't the money belong to both of you? Shouldn't you have equal say-so about how it's spent?"

She turned palms up. "If he's opposed to our getting help for Georgie, then I'm not sure what I can do."

I was scared and I was mad. Grown-ups are screwheads!

"Well, I know what I can do!" I got up from the table. "Mrs. T. will be glad to help if—"

"Don't you dare ask her!" Mom fairly leaped from her chair. It scraped loudly on the tile floor. "This is none of her business!"

"She's no busybody, Mom—"

"I don't care! Let me handle this myself."

"But, Mom, don't you realize we might have to ask someone for help, or Georgie will . . ."

Her face lost its shape, like paper in water. Tears filled her eyes.

"Neal, I'm doing the best I can."

The air hummed with our terror. Maybe in her shoes I couldn't do any better, but you always expect more of your mom than you do of yourself.

My shoulders slumped. "All right. I won't ask Mrs. T." Yet, I added to myself.

The doorbell rang. Mom looked up at the clock and sighed. Automatically she began to rearrange her face along pleasanter lines. I hated to see it.

"I'll go," I said. "I'm going up to do my homework now, anyway."

"It's for your father, I'm sure," she said.

"Yeah. Makes you wonder why he won't go to the door himself, doesn't it?" I chafed as I went along the hallway. It would be so easy for him to walk out of his study and open the front door, but he wouldn't do it in a million years as long as someone else in the house would run interference for him. He likes people to be ushered in to him, like he was the king and they were his loyal subjects.

I don't know who I was expecting to see on the other side of the door, but when I opened it and saw Mr. Mac, I went weak inside.

"How do, Neal?" He bobbed his head once. "Is your dad home?"

"Y-yes, sir."

"Wonder if I could speak with him?"

"I . . . yes, sir." I opened the screen door and stood back. "Come in. I'll get him."

Panic rose and scrambled my brain. Oh, Jesus! It was going to happen even sooner than I had anticipated. Mr. Mac walked past me into the hall and stood there expectantly. Somehow in that space he seemed larger than usual.

"Is this about today?" I blurted.

He frowned. "Today?"

"Me being in church." I spoke rapidly and softly. "Because if it is, you don't really need to talk with Dad about it. I'm careful to lock up, and I never use the lights or turn up the heat."

He gave me a thoughtful look. "No, it isn't about today."

What then? I stood there like some kind of idiot, at a loss for what to say next.

"I won't mention to your dad that I saw you in the church," he said. "It's not what I came for."

"Thanks," I said, much relieved. "I appreciate it."

I wanted to explain that I really hadn't done anything wrong, even though I was acting like someone who had. I wanted to beg him not to tell anyone else, but it was too complicated. One answer always leads to new questions.

"Now may I see him?" he said patiently.

"I'm sorry. Come in the living room and take a seat."

He followed me into the room, but he didn't sit down. Under the light his thinning hair glistened. He rocked back and forth from heel to toe, his hands joined behind him like a man about to give a speech. His solemn manner indicated serious business.

"Er . . . just a second, Neal," he said as I was about to leave. "Before you go I'd like to ask you something."

"Yes, sir?" I was immediately on guard.

"Does your dad seem to feel good these days?"

I looked at him hard, trying to see behind the bland gaze to the reason for his question.

"Well, sure—he's not sick or anything."

"He hasn't seemed particularly upset lately?"

I shrugged, caught between what I knew and what I could tell. "No more than usual." I gave a nervous little laugh. "You know how parents get upset with their kids."

He nodded. "All right. I just wondered."

I came back into the room. "Why? What's the matter?"

"I don't know that anything's the matter," he said. "Maybe you could fetch your dad now."

When I tapped on the study door Dad opened it immediately, as though he'd been standing there all that time waiting for his cue.

"Mr. Mac's here."

He nodded. "Show him in here. You might ask your mother to fix us some refreshments."

"I'll do it. She's tired."

I showed Mr. Mac to the study and went back to the kitchen. Mom was hanging up her apron.

"It's Mr. Mac," I said, taking a can of lemonade concentrate out of the freezer. "To see Dad, of course."

She yawned. Then noting that I'd gotten out a pitcher and spoon, she spoke sharply. "What are you doing? I've told you a hundred times not to come back in the kitchen and mess up after I've put everything away!"

"Dad wanted refreshments served. I'm fixing it so you won't have to."

There was a little pause. "Thanks," she said, softening. "Sorry I'm so crabby."

"I guess you have reason to be crabby," I said, not looking at her. "I'll leave everything shipshape, I promise."

"All right. And, Neal—I'll speak with your father tonight about the counseling. I promise."

I did look at her then. My smile was one-sided. "You've got guts," I said. She shook her head and went out. In a few seconds I heard the bedroom door close. I found a serving tray and some napkins, put ice in the glass, and poured the lemonade. I wiped up the spills and washed the stirring spoon. This kind of promise was easy to keep.

The study door was closed, but I could hear their voices. I stood there a moment, holding the tray, while I tried to figure how I was going to knock.

"That's incredible!" I heard Dad burst out. "There's no truth to it at all! You know there's not!"

Mr. Mac replied in a lower voice. I had to strain to hear something about "all over town."

"I can't imagine!" Dad's voice shook. "Why would anyone say that?"

Mr. Mac, murmuring again. Then Dad. My mouth was dry. I held the tray so tightly my muscles ached. Should I go away or should I knock? What news had Mr. Mac brought?

"Well, I wouldn't get too upset," I heard Mr. Mac say soothingly. "I didn't know if you'd gotten wind of it. My main reason for coming over was just to let you know that if there was some . . . er . . . problem, we folks in the church want to help out in whatever way we can. . . ."

"There's no problem!" Dad's fury was unmistakable. "No problem at all except in the head of the . . . the unbalanced person who started those stories."

I kicked at the study door.

"Come in!" Dad barked.

Balancing the tray on one hand, I turned the knob and pushed the door open. I hoped I looked like I hadn't heard a word. Mr. Mac was in the black leather chair, and Dad was sitting at the desk. He was very pale. His hair seemed more unruly than ever.

"Here's the lemonade," I said. "Where would you like me to put it?"

It seemed to take a tremendous effort for him to think about the question. He motioned to the desk, and I cleared a place for the tray.

"Anything else?" I asked, backing toward the door. Mr. Mac watched me carefully.

"No. No, that's all. Thank you." I had never seen Dad so distraught, certainly not in front of a church member. I said my good nights and went out, closing the door behind me. I stood in the hall trying to decide what to do. Should I warn Mom that something was up, or just let her find out from Dad? Should I hang around and eavesdrop some more, or—

"I'll be going now," Mr. Mac said from the other side of the door. "Like I say, don't let this thing upset you too much. You know how it is in a little town like Gideon. People don't have enough to keep them busy, and things like this get started almost by accident. They don't mean to do harm, most of the time."

I moved quickly then, and was crouched at the top of the stairs in the dark when the two men came out of the study.

"Thank you for coming," Dad said hollowly. "I appreciate your concern."

"I'll do all I can, Preacher, to assure folks there's no truth to the tales. I believe it'll blow over soon. Good night, now."

Mr. Mac went out. Dad closed the front door firmly behind him and then sagged against it. The downstairs bedroom door opened, and I heard Mom call him.

"Richard? What is it?"

"I wish I knew!" he choked. "God, do I ever wish I knew!"

She came quickly up the hall. "Tell me. What's wrong?"

"Someone has started rumors about me, Lou—that I'm about to be asked to leave. That I'm suffering from all kinds of emotional problems."

"Richard! Who?"

"I don't know." They moved into the living room, and I had to listen hard to hear. "Mac was getting it from so many different sources he . . . he decided to come here and see whether—"

He couldn't finish the sentence. His voice was high and anguished, full of shock and disbelief that this could have happened. In front of people he was so smooth and calm.

It was weird. What irony, to think that someone had started a rumor based on nothing they knew about, whereas Aileen and I could've filled everyone's ears for years with the truth, and probably no one would have believed us. Maybe it was cosmic justice, but the timing was bad.

I got up and went to my room. For a long time I sat at my desk and stared into space. I couldn't begin to concentrate on homework. When Mom had told me about getting help for Georgie, I had actually begun to hope, but now that this had happened we could just forget it. Dad would rather die than be seen anywhere near a psychiatric clinic now!

CHAPTER 15

When I went down to breakfast next morning, Dad was already sitting at the table. His hair was uncombed, his eyes puffy. The skin of his face seemed to have lost its underpinnings. Mom moved in and out of the dining room, putting things on the table. She spoke to me, but her expression was closed and locked. I was pretty sure that meant that last night's circumstances had kept her from keeping her promise. I had to pretend to both of them that I didn't know what was up.

Soon Aileen and Georgie came in. He seemed more relaxed than last night, probably because of all the attention he'd been getting from her. But when he caught sight of Dad, he seemed to become smaller, less visible, right before our eyes. He slipped into his chair, scarcely moving it at all.

"What's the matter, Dad?" Aileen came straight to the point. "You look sort of under the weather."

"Under siege is more like it." His tone was subdued, lacking any of the pick-a-fight quality it usually had. That in itself was disturbing. We waited until Mom had taken her place and Dad had said a distracted blessing. When the scrambled eggs were being passed around, Aileen asked again.

Dad sighed and put his head in his hands. I noted his elbows on the table and wondered what Georgie would think of that.

"Mac was here last night. What he told me came as a tremendous shock—totally unexpected. Someone . . . in this town has started rumors to the effect that I . . . that I'm not emotionally stable." He lifted his head and looked at us when he spoke, as though hoping to hear an outburst of denial from around the table. When it didn't come, his voice took on a note of desperation. "I can't imagine why anyone would do this, or how such lies could take root and spread. Why, I'm no different than I've ever been! Why now, all of a sudden? I asked Mac if he'd seen anything in my behavior to suggest that I wasn't emotionally stable, and he said of course not. But he still came here to check it out."

He shook his head, still not able to comprehend what had happened. I felt sorry for him.

"Well," said Aileen, ever practical, "maybe the best thing to do is to ride it out. Ignore what's being said—pretend you haven't heard a thing. If you get self-conscious, you may start acting peculiar, and that'll only make things worse."

Dad's face darkened. "That's easy to say, but I have to be with people constantly. Who can tell what they're thinking?"

"Does Mr. Mac have any ideas about how it started?" I asked.

He shook his head. "It seems to have surfaced rather suddenly in several different places during the past few days."

"Just what are they saying?" asked Aileen.

"I'm not certain—Mac was reluctant to repeat everything he'd heard. He did say that there was talk among people of other denominations that I was about to be asked to step down as pastor of this church. He says he squelched that. But the other tale is that I'm very close to a nervous breakdown, and that I'm having family troubles."

Mom looked at him quickly. He didn't seem to give any special weight to "family troubles." Probably he didn't think he had any. I felt the floor go out from under me. Who besides us knew about our family troubles? Mrs. T., of course, but I knew she'd never tell. I looked at Mom, at Aileen, at Georgie. Who did they talk to? Mom had no one—of that I was pretty certain. Georgie had Captain Perry, but Captain couldn't be understood by anyone else, and besides, I doubted that Georgie talked much about what actually went on in our household. He'd be too terrified. As for Aileen, I suppose she's filled Pete's ears with a lot of our junk over the past year. There's certainly no love lost between him and Dad, since Pete hasn't been welcome at our house. But somehow it seemed out of character for Pete to try to get back at Dad in such an underhanded way.

"What's the matter, Neal?" Mom asked.

"I . . . nothing."

"Do you know something?" Dad peered closely at me. I became uneasy.

"No," I said. "I was just trying to think who might . . . but I can't . . . I don't know."

"In any case," Mom said quietly, "none of us has any control over what other people say about us. Or over what they choose to believe about us. Sometimes I think we spend far too much energy trying to make sure they believe nothing but the best. The Sloans aren't perfect, by a long shot."

"That may be true, Lou," Dad said, "but I'm not crazy either! Rest assured, I intend to get to the bottom of this."

What a useless exercise, I thought, but I knew better than to say it. I kept my eyes on my plate and ate in silence. So did everyone else. The atmosphere was very glum.

"You three will be late for school if you don't hurry," Mom said a few minutes later. "Georgie, Aileen is going to walk with you this morning—understand?" Her eyes said, "And no funny business." He nodded obediently. We got up and started out of the dining room.

"Wait," said Dad. He, too, got up. "If you hear anything . . . negative . . . at school, you should state very clearly that there's no truth to it."

"But, Dad, what good—" Aileen began.

He stopped her with a wave of his hand. "If we don't put a stop to these tales, there's no telling how far they'll go. Just remember that."

We left the house soon afterward, Georgie walking between

Aileen and me so we could both keep an eye on him. Mom had filled Aileen in on his disappearing act the day before. Occasionally he would look up at me, then at Aileen, blinking behind the glasses.

"It's weird, isn't it?" Aileen said when we had gone a little way. "He's so perfect in public!"

"Yes. It's a mystery. I mean, we're the only people who know what he's really like."

She sighed. "It's tempting, you know, not to defend him. Just to let people believe that he's not emotionally stable."

"Hey, keep your voice down!" I said. "That's putting it a little strongly, don't you think?"

"Well, he has his moments," she said. "I know what he was like that night when I was going to meet Pete and he yelled at me and sent me to my room. If that's stable, then I don't ever want to see unstable."

"You don't think Pete had anything to do with these rumors, do you?"

Her eyes widened, and then she began to laugh. "Pete? God, no! He threatened to come to our house and punch Dad out when he found out what happened, but when I convinced him it wouldn't make my life any easier, he cooled down. No, Pete isn't a gossip."

"That's what I thought," I said. "I just wish I could figure out where it started."

"What difference does it make? The question is, what do we do—you and Georgie and I? Do we protest, or do we allow the truth to get out—that he's as flawed as we are?"

"Aileen, don't talk like that—you make me nervous!"

She shrugged. "Well, frankly, I think it'd do Dad a lot of good to show people his warts. It would take some of the pressure off him, and us too."

"Maybe so. But you can't expect someone who's been image-conscious for as many years as he has to make any sudden, over-night change."

In fact, I thought glumly, it was probably expecting too much to hope for any change at all. Still, the shock of the rumors had seemed to make Dad less guarded. I remembered his elbows on the table, and he had actually admitted that he was upset.

She giggled. "Well, Dad would have to go really bonkers to make a worse reputation for himself than *I* have here in Gideon, and I've survived. He can take hope—it's not the end of the world!"

I couldn't help laughing. "You're impossible, Aileen!"

"Maybe so. But I'm real."

"You know something?" I said. "You're the only person in our family to hide the *good* side of yourself."

She gave me an affectionate smile. "Thanks for seeing that I have a good side. I need reminding every so often that I'm not completely bad—it's the only way I'll be able to get out of the mess I've gotten myself into."

"Well, I'd ask what you plan to do, but the last time I did that you nearly bit my head off."

"Sorry. It was because you were right—I was cutting off my nose to spite my face. I'm going to talk to Mr. Hampton to see whether I can go to summer school and pass the English. I still won't be able to enroll in college in the fall, but I think I can get into Tech. The sooner I get out of Gideon for good, the better. As much as I hate to admit it, Dad's forcing me to study three hours a day is paying off."

"What about Pete?"

"Oh, Pete will find his way. He'll get bored. Actually, we've been good for each other. He knows I'm not perfectly good, and I know he's not perfectly awful. The problem for both of us is that we can't be who we really are in Gideon—people have already decided who they want us to be."

"Yeah, that's what I think, too." I stared into the distance, thinking of myself playing jazz in Gideon. "Do you suppose—"

"Suppose what?"

"Do you suppose nobody in Gideon is who they really are?"

"No!" Georgie shouted at the top of his lungs.

Aileen and I were struck dumb. He'd been so quiet I'd all but forgotten he was with us.

"*Don't say that!*" He stopped in his tracks and stomped so hard he dropped his book bag. I tried to think what I'd said to get him so upset.

"You told me you were Real!" he wailed, on the verge of tears. "Aileen just said she was Real, too. Captain is Real!"

Aileen's eyes were dark with worry. I put my books on the ground and knelt beside him, hugging him close.

"Georgie, you misunderstood. I meant . . . something else."

"What's he talking about, anyway?" Aileen asked. I got to my feet, dusting the knees of my jeans.

"It's just something we talked about once," I said. "Maybe he'll tell you about it sometime, huh, Georgie?"

He pretended not to hear. We'd almost reached the school grounds by that time. "I'm going to my room by myself," he said.

"It's O.K. by me," said Aileen.

"Well, it's not O.K. by me," I said firmly. "We're all three going."

"I'll go by myself," Georgie said stubbornly.

"No dice, buddy." We locked eyes. He gave in then and allowed us to walk him to his classroom. Miss Harvey seemed surprised to see both of us with him. I could see the questions in her eyes, but she didn't ask them, just gave Georgie an extra-large welcome and sent him to his seat.

"Poor little guy," Aileen said when we left the elementary building and headed for the high school wing. "I realized last night I haven't paid him much attention lately."

"None of us has unless he does something wrong. That's the problem." I started to tell her about the psychiatric clinic in Hatboro, but decided there was too much to explain now. Maybe I'd tell her this afternoon.

In homeroom and English class everything seemed normal enough. Perry Green lent me a pencil when my pen ran out of ink, and Mickey Lutz begged me to let her copy my notes. She always does that right before a test. No one seemed to be looking at me funny or whispering things behind my back. I was about as invisible as a familiar piece of furniture that has been sitting in the same place for a long time.

Then Mr. Hampton called me up to his desk.

"You don't have to do another paper, Neal, now that I know about the one you wrote. I kept it, even though it's in Pete's handwriting with his misspelling. It's an interesting paper."

"Thank you," I said.

"What I liked about it," he went on, "was the feeling that you weren't just reciting facts about Monk, or someone else's opinions about his musical style. I had the distinct impression that you knew what you were talking about."

The floor under my feet seemed to shift. I didn't know what to do with my arms. I stuck my hands in my pockets. "I'm . . . glad it sounded that way."

"I have a recording you might like to listen to sometime," he said. "I heard Monk play once in New York when I was about your age."

My heart leaped. "Really? In person? I—" Then I knew by the gleam in his eye that I'd given myself away. Damn him, nosing around, anyhow! "Well," I said, making my voice bored, "yeah, it'd be interesting to hear sometime."

I went back to my desk, feeling exposed, like yesterday when Mr. Mac found me playing in church. God, I hoped Mr. Mac and Mr. Hampton never had occasion to talk to each other! I sat and stared for a while at some words on a page, but I couldn't think. Maybe it feels like this when you commit a crime and don't cover your tracks well enough. When you see people start putting two and two together, you know it's just a matter of time before they come knocking at your door.

The bell rang for the end of the period. I went out with the surge of bodies, intent on not looking at Mr. Hampton.

Pete was standing by my locker.

"H'lo," I said. I wondered if he'd try to keep me from opening it or otherwise cause trouble. He didn't reply to my greeting, just kept looking like he was waiting for something. An apology, maybe. I had a sudden inspiration.

"Look," I said, opening the locker and putting the English books inside, "how much is it costing you to fix your boat and pay for the repairs to Mrs. Burney's pier?"

"What's it to you?"

"Well, I didn't like the insinuations about Mrs. Talbot, but I overreacted. I'm not sorry for getting mad, but I'm sorry for the damage. I'll go halves."

He gave me a long, frowning look. "What is this? 'Fraid you gonna lose your good-guy reputation or somethin'?"

Anger began to burn in me, slow and deep. I kept my voice low so it wouldn't shake. "No. I'm just saying I'll take my share of the responsibility."

"In that case, I'd say you ought to pay for the whole thing." He folded his arms across his chest and grinned. It wasn't friendly. "If you hadn't've flew off the handle, nothin' would've happened."

"I'll pay half," I said. I turned back to the locker and started getting out books for the next class. "Think it over."

In the next instant he grabbed my arm and spun me around, slamming me against the locker. It knocked the wind out of me. Before I could let go of the books, his fist connected with my jaw. My head jerked back and banged against metal.

I reached out blindly and grabbed—shirt, flesh, greasy hair, whatever I could get my hands on. The next thing I knew we were rolling on the floor among feet and books, trying to kill each other.

Somebody pulled us apart. I was yanked to my feet from behind and heard Mr. Hampton's voice in my ear telling me to cool it. Coach Sardis had Pete in an armlock. When things began to focus, I saw we were surrounded by faces several rows deep with every possible expression, from shock to simple amusement.

"All right!" Coach Sardis bellowed. "Y'all get to class or you're gonna be counted tardy!" The bell rang to punctuate the order, and the crowd melted away, muttering and giggling, leaving Pete and me and the two men.

"What got into you two?" Coach Sardis said. "You could be suspended for *days* for fightin' in school!"

I kept my eyes on the floor. Books and papers lay scattered about.

"Are those yours?" Mr. Hampton asked.

"Yes, sir."

"Pick them up then. Both of you have to see Mr. Thompson."

My stomach lurched. I picked up the books and papers, aware of Pete's dirty sneakers shoving some of the papers toward me. I clenched my teeth to keep from yelling at him to keep his nasty feet off my stuff.

Coach Sardis took us down to the office. "You sit there, Pete, and you sit there, Neal, and don't y'all even look at each other, you hear me?"

We both mumbled something, and he disappeared into Mr. Thompson's inner office. Mrs. Glasser, the secretary, pursed her lips, disapproving of us. My jaw had begun to feel stiff and sore, along with the spot on the back of my head that had hit the locker.

Pete had a long scratch mark down the side of his face and some blood at the corner of his mouth. I hoped he ached as much as I did, the turd!

Coach Sardis came back and signaled us into the office. "I got to go back to class," he said. "I already told Mr. Thompson what I saw. Get on in there."

We stood before Mr. Thompson's desk like prisoners before the judge. He did not look very merciful. He leaned back in the swivel chair and regarded us sternly.

"Well, boys, just about the last thing I said to you before you left this office yesterday was no fighting here at school. Do you happen to remember that?"

"Yes, sir," I muttered, looking at his desk top.

"You, Pete?"

"Yeah, I guess."

"You guess? Did you hear me say it or not?"

Long pause. Then, "Yes, I heard you say it."

"I suppose each one of you is going to tell me the other started it."

"Well, he did start it," Pete began. "He came up to me and—"

Mr. Thompson stopped him. "I don't want to hear it. When Coach Sardis got there you were both into it. We will *not* tolerate this kind of rowdiness in the school from anyone—is that clear?"

"Yes, sir." I barely opened my mouth.

"Pete, you don't seem to hear so well. It takes you too long to answer questions."

"Yes, *sir*!"

Mr. Thompson's eyes glinted steel. "In-school suspension for both of you, starting right now. Neal, I'm calling your parents to inform them and ask them to come to school with you tomorrow morning. Meanwhile, both of you go straight to the detention hall."

CHAPTER 16

So far as I know, Dad has never darkened the door of the principal's office since we've lived in Gideon. Any troubles that arose between our teachers and us have been handled by Mom. Nothing ever went so far that a trip to the office was required. Not even Aileen's escapades have called for a conference with the principal. Yet here we were—Dad, Mom, and I—stuffed into a space in Mr. Thompson's office so small we could barely move without bumping knees. Mr. Thompson had retreated behind the desk, which he seemed to be using as a shield, while the rest of us made a ragged semicircle in metal folding chairs brought in for the occasion.

Mr. Thompson cleared his throat, running his fingers absently over the desk's surface as if to assure himself that it was solid and would hold up under attack.

"I'm sorry for the circumstances that prompted this meeting, Mr. and Mrs. Sloan," he began. "*Very* sorry. Neal has generally been a responsible student. He's never given us any trouble before the last couple of days."

"The last couple of days?" Mom echoed. "You mean that the fight yesterday wasn't his first infraction?"

Mr. Thompson blinked at the word. People in Gideon tend toward a more basic vocabulary.

"Well, let me put it this way. He was involved in an earlier . . . unpleasantness, but so far as I could determine, that wasn't of his own making. However, I regret to say it was with the same person as yesterday's incident—Pete Cauthin."

Neither of my parents made any attempt to diguise their dislike of Pete. However, Mr. Thompson did not let on whether or not he knew anything about the relationship between Aileen and Pete. "Monday I warned both boys that I wouldn't tolerate any disruption of school routine from them. I told them they'd have to settle their conflicts somewhere else. I thought it was clear. Neal certainly agreed there'd be no more fighting."

Three pairs of eyes turned in my direction. I looked at a spot on my right knee. Since Mom and Dad had gotten the call from Mr. Thompson yesterday morning, life at home had been pretty miserable. Instead of raking me over the coals as I had expected him to do, Dad maintained a stony silence. Once in a while I'd catch him giving me that now-look-what-you've-done look. Mom was exasperated with me and didn't try to hide it. I stayed in my room a lot. Coming to school was almost a relief, even though I still had to get through this conference.

"Neal's previous record of good behavior is a plus," Mr. Thompson said, talking about me as though I were not even there. "I think continuing his suspension through today will be enough punishment for him, although I may have to be more severe with Pete. Frankly, I didn't try to find out how the fight began—it's human nature for each person to try to justify himself. Coach Sardis said they were fighting with equal enthusiasm. I hope this will be the last time Neal is involved in something of this sort. I called the conference in the hope that you'll use your influence with him."

"That's good of you," Dad said coldly, "but I'm not sure what influence we have with Neal any more. At the rate he's going, he's becoming another Pete Cauthin."

Mom looked at him in sharp surprise.

"I've concluded," he went on, "that one does the best one can in the matter of bringing up children. One tries to set a good example. But if a young person chooses in spite of that to act irresponsibly—"

"Well, now, Mr. Sloan, I don't want you to get the wrong idea." Mr. Thompson tried to be soothing. "Neal is no juvenile delinquent. He's really the only person who's been hurt by this incident. We're not talking about destruction of property or human life. I'm just interested in seeing that he won't get into bad behavior patterns. I thought—"

"If he's gotten into bad behavior patterns, it's not my fault," Dad interrupted, leaning forward in his chair. "I've done everything I could to point his life in the right direction. I've done that with *all* my children. . . ." He let the words hang. I could hear the part he wasn't saying: "But you can see how they've turned out."

I couldn't believe he was acting this way after all his worry about what people thought of him. He didn't seem to have any idea about how he was coming across to Mr. Thompson.

"Mr. Thompson isn't blaming you for anything, Richard," Mom said. "He only wants our cooperation in helping Neal keep his school record clean."

Mr. Thompson nodded, greatly relieved. "That's right. I don't expect Neal to be a chronic troublemaker—I really don't." He pulled a handkerchief from his pocket and dabbed at his forehead.

"Well, then, did you just call us in to see how I'd react to Neal's being punished?" Dad asked. "Was that the point?"

"Richard, Mr. Thompson is doing exactly what he's supposed to do in cases like this." Mom spoke firmly in a low voice. "Whenever there's a suspension, parents have to come to school as a matter of policy. I personally appreciate Mr. Thompson's concern." And, her tone implied, you'd better do the same.

The next few seconds lasted several hours. I had a bad case of the dry mouth.

"Well, perhaps you're right," Dad said finally. His mouth was stiff, his manner unyielding. Only his words were correct. He stood up abruptly, and Mr. Thompson, taken unaware, scrambled to his feet. Dad put out his hand. "Thank you for calling this to ur attention. I hope it won't happen again." Then he turned and walked out of the office without a nod in anyone's direction.

My own embarrassment was so deep I couldn't feel it any more. Mr. Thompson didn't know what had hit him, and Mom's face was like wax. She shook the principal's hand too. "I'm sorry," she said. "I'll talk with Neal."

"Thank you, Mrs. Sloan. I hope you understand it's Neal I'm concerned about—not the school rules." He looked at me. "See your mother out, Neal, and then come back here before you go to the detention hall, please."

We went out into the hall. Dad was nowhere in sight. Mom took a deep breath and turned to me, shaking her head.

"I'm sorry about all this," I mumbled. "Maybe if I'd—"

"Don't!" she interrupted. "Tell me, what's wrong between you and Pete? Does it have anything to do with Aileen?"

"No. We had a . . . disagreement about something. I offered to settle up and he took it the wrong way. From now on, I'm just staying out of his orbit."

Mom sighed again. "I'm astounded at the way your father acted in there. That sort of thing isn't going to help matters at all!"

"Who's going to tell him?" I said. "He won't listen to anyone. The more paranoid he gets, the more peculiar he acts. If he doesn't watch it, people will start believing what they hear about him, and it'll be his own fault."

She rubbed her forehead as though to help herself think clearly. "I'm not sure what to do next," she said, more to herself than to me, "but after this episode if I don't do something, then I'm crazy!" She gave me a pat on the arm. "Go back to the office and see what Mr. Thompson wants. I'll see you this afternoon when you get home. And try not to worry."

That was a laugh. I went back to the office feeling drained and shaky. I wanted to walk out of the place and never come back, but there had already been too much trouble on my account.

"You can go straight in, Neal," Mrs. Glasser said. "Mr. Thompson's waiting for you."

He was standing by the window looking out. When I entered,

he came around to my side of the desk. "Neal, I'm sorry your father got upset. I'm afraid he misunderstood."

"He doesn't want us to do anything wrong," I said. "He'll get over it."

Mr. Thompson bent over the desk and wrote a note. "Take this to detention hall, and when you return to classes tomorrow, be sure that all your teachers see it."

"Yes, sir."

"And, Neal—is there anything I can do to resolve the problem between you and Pete?"

I shook my head. "I don't think so."

"Is he bullying you?"

"He's not big enough to bully me."

He almost smiled. "Well, I just want you to know I'm not out to get you. If I can do something, I'd like to know about it."

"Yes, sir. Thanks." I folded the note and went out.

Walking home that afternoon in the warm sun, I felt that I had accidentally stumbled into someone else's life—the soft greenery did not fit mine. There's something cruel about bright weather when everything inside a person is dark and gloomy. The sky should have the courtesy to cloud over at such a time.

I've never worried about going bonkers—I guess I thought I wasn't the type, but now I was beginning to wonder. Not since I began the music two years ago had I been faced with the prospect of going for days on end with no instrument to play. Music is as much a part of me as eating and sleeping. There's nothing I can do *instead* of it to ease the craving. It crowds out everything else, especially when reality is so bleak. Like in the detention hall—I couldn't keep my mind on the work I was assigned. It kept drifting to music. I can't *do* jazz on paper! I hear it so clearly in my head, but I have to *really* hear it.

"I'm gonna die," I muttered aloud, wishing it were the truth. Sometimes staying alive is harder. I reached up and felt the lump on the back of my head, where it had hit the locker. It was still sore to touch.

I didn't hear Georgie until he fell into step beside me. I should be used to his sudden appearances by now, but I'm not. My heart skipped and then settled down to its regular beat again.

"For Pete's sake, quit sneaking up on people like that!" I said. "It scares the hell out of me every time you do it."

Startled by my ferociousness, he slowed down and hung back. "I thought you saw m-me," he said, beginning to stutter. "Y-you l-looked r-right at me."

"Oh, never mind!" I grumped. "Come on. It's O.K. I'm just not in a very good mood."

"Did something bad happen today?"

"Yes, as a matter of fact." I looked down at him, and I guess he thought I was accusing him.

"I didn't m-mean f-for anything b-bad t-to happen." The pulse throbbed in his throat just under the jawline.

"You didn't do anything. *I* did."

I told him about the fight in the hall yesterday, my two days of in-school suspension, and the conference with Mom and Dad. I talked loud because the lump in my throat was pressing so hard I was afraid I couldn't make sounds if I didn't bellow.

"Is Dad mad?" Georgie asked. "He doesn't like for us to . . to . . ."

"To bring negative attention to the family name," I finished for him.

He nodded. " 'Specially now," he said in a hushed voice. "Now that people think he's crazy."

I looked at him quickly, but his face was impassive.

"I don't know that people think he's crazy," I said. "At least not yet. If he acts like he did this morning in Mr. Thompson's office, though, they may begin to think so."

"Who do you s'pose started the rumor that he was crazy?" he persisted.

"Look, Georgie, Mr. Mac used words like 'emotionally un-stable' and 'problems.' Nobody but Dad said 'crazy.' And to answer your question, I haven't the slightest idea."

He walked along beside me, clutching his books tightly. After a while he asked, "What do you think will happen when Dad finds out who the person is?"

"Oh, I don't know. Nothing, probably. He'll fume and rant around the house, but when he comes face to face with them, he'll be the soul of Christian charity—to make them look bad and him look good."

"You know what I bet?" he said in a hushed voice. "I bet some other people are finding out he's not Real. He's not going to fool them any more!"

"You'd like that, wouldn't you?" I said.

He glanced at me guiltily, then looked away. I probed a little. "Do you still think Mom is False?' "

He seemed troubled by the question. His small face screwed into a frown. "I can't be sure. Sometimes she seems False, and sometimes she seems Real. Maybe she's pretending to be False so he won't hurt her. Or maybe she's pretending to be Real to trick me."

As before when he got on this subject, his eyes gleamed with eerie excitement.

"Georgie," I said carefully, "we're all real—Mom, Aileen, me, you—even Dad. Maybe we pretend to each other too much. We don't *act* who we really are. Maybe a better word for False is phony."

He stiffened and moved away from me a little, as though he feared I would contaminate him. He shook his head.

"If I believed that, I might get caught."

I wanted him to trust me, but I didn't want to say anything that would encourage his weird fantasy. "So you still think about being replaced," I said casually.

He went white, and for a second I thought he might faint. He shifted the books nervously. "Sometimes."

We were almost home by then. He seemed anxious to get there. I, on the other hand, could think of nothing I'd like better than never going there again.

"I'm going over to Mrs. T.'s for a little while before I come home," I told him. "Tell Mom if she asks. Don't make up any tales, though."

He nodded, and we parted ways. As I crossed the street to Mrs. T.'s, I felt like a pilgrim about to reach Mecca at last.

CHAPTER 17

For two years I've made it a practice not to hang around Mrs. T.'s house during the time of day when she has other pupils. Besides not wanting anyone to make the connection between me and music, I can't stand bad piano playing—it drives me up the wall. Today, though, it seemed to me that bad playing would be more bearable than going home to face another kind of music.

The steps to the side deck smelled of seasoned wood. I sat down there, hidden from the street by some bushes, and tried to sort things out. Inside Mrs. T.'s house someone's fingers stumbled miserably through half a dozen keyboard exercises.

Blessedly, the playing stopped, and in a few minutes a plump little girl about Georgie's age came out, clutching an armful of music books. When she saw me she hesitated, not sure whether to take the chance of walking by me. I must've looked big, even sitting down.

"Hi!" I said.

"Hello." She looked at me warily.

"I heard you," I said. "You play pretty good." I crossed my fingers for the lie. Her face relaxed into a smug little smile.

"Thank you. Do you take music lessons too?"

I kept my fingers crossed. "No. Mrs. Talbot's a friend of mine. I came to visit."

She passed by me on the other side of the steps, holding the railing carefully with her free hand. "You can go in now," she said primly. "I've finished."

I watched her walk away, tickled by her self-important air. I remembered being seven and believing that someday I was going to be famous and admired. I carried the secret around inside, and it made me tough and maybe even a little bit conceited. When had I quit believing? Would I ever get it back?

I walked across the deck and let myself in at the side door. Mrs. T. saw me before I saw her.

"Neal! What are you doing here at this hour?" She wore one of her teaching costumes, a multicolored caftan that is about as non-Gideon as an outfit can be.

"I could come later if it's a bad time."

"It's perfect. No one is scheduled until four o'clock. We have about thirty minutes. Leslie just left."

"Yeah, I know. I heard the last of her lesson." I frowned and she laughed.

"I'll fix something cold to drink. Play for me."

I didn't wait for a second invitation. The piano bench was still warm from Leslie's backside when I slid onto it and began to play. Music poured instantly from my fingers, as though the energy had been stored there waiting for the touch of keys. Moments like this I love myself. I am good. I am wonderful! I'm amazed that fingers, mind, and feelings all come together to produce this great sound, and it's coming out of *me*. How it happens I don't know. But who cares? It happens!

I played and played. After a while I realized that sweat was trickling down my sides and my shoulders ached. I looked up and caught Mrs. T.'s eye across the length of the open piano. She shook her head.

"Oh, Neal, Neal, Neal." The words were admiring and despairing all at once. "What will I do with you?"

I let my hands drop into my lap, feeling drained and peaceful.

"Do with me?" I repeated stupidly "You don't have to do anything with me except let me get to this piano often enough to keep my sanity. Another couple of hours without it and I think I'd have done something really crazy."

I stood up to stretch, and she handed me a glass of lemonade. The ice had nearly melted.

"Say, how long did I—"

"Almost an hour," she said, answering my question before I could finish it.

"But you have a lesson at four!"

"I telephoned and canceled it. I figured you had a reason for being here. Come on—we'll sit on the deck and watch the river while we talk."

I followed her through the large double doors to the rear deck. Tall pines near the house shaded us from the afternoon sun. We sat in deck chairs, and I propped my feet on the railing. The placid river reminded me of a large woman who has grown accustomed to moving slowly. It seemed a shame to bring trouble into such a peaceful place, and for a long time I wouldn't say anything. But then I began to talk, haltingly at first, then in a rush of words. So much had happened in a few days that I felt I had been thrown feet-first into a speeded-up film. I told her about the rumors someone had started and how Dad's fear was making him act strange. I told about the fight with Pete, being suspended, and the conference with my folks in Mr. Thompson's office. I told about Georgie's mysterious vanishing act and his teacher's concern. Finally I told her what had happened at the church Monday afternoon.

"That was the worst thing." I said. "Getting caught by Mr. Mac. There's no telling how long he stood there listening to me before I knew he was anywhere around. It's only a matter of time before the whole damn town knows."

"Did he like what he heard?" she asked curiously.

"I don't know," I shrugged. "He didn't make fun, and he didn't say anything about the kind of music I was playing." I stopped and thought a minute. "Hey, that's weird, isn't it? I mean, that piano used to belong to Mr. Mac, and it's in a church sanctuary, but he didn't say anything about my playing jazz instead of hymns."

Mrs. T. chuckled. "That *is* weird. Maybe Mac is a closet jazz man himself."

I had to laugh at that, but then a sudden thought sobered me. "You know, Mrs. T., if that had been Dad he would've grabbed my arm and jerked me off the piano bench. He would've been infuriated."

"Why?"

I turned and looked at her, puzzled. "I don't *know* why, but I'm pretty sure that's what he would've done."

I looked out at the river again. "The truth is, I could handle other people here knowing about my piano playing. Mostly they'd ignore me. It might even be that somewhere around here there are some jazz freaks just as hungry for it as I am. What I dread most is Dad's finding out. He'd move in on me. He'd insist we get a piano for me to practice on, but then he'd start monitoring what I played. Maybe he couldn't keep me from playing jazz, but if he made enough sarcastic remarks about it, pretty soon I'd . . . well, nobody likes to see what they love made fun of." I sighed. "I hope Mr. Mac keeps his mouth shut, but that's just wishful thinking."

"It's a problem," she acknowledged, "but maybe there's a solution in it. If Mac does spill the beans, you can be open about coming here. We can set up a practice schedule—two hours a day after my teaching sessions are over. You won't have to make up excuses."

"That sounds good, but Dad has a one-track mind. I'd hate to see his righteous wrath fall on your head on my account."

"Well, that's a bridge we can cross when we have to." She was silent for a while, thinking. "So much has happened in a short time. How can you be so calm?"

"I don't know that I'm calm. Numb is more like it." I sat up and leaned forward in the chair, draping my arms over the railing. The veins on the backs of my hands filled and knotted until suddenly they looked like the hands of a very old man. "Everything is upside down."

"Or right side up at long last," she said. "Perhaps the hidden things are coming to the surface. What's real won't hide any more. Bad as it may seem, I think that's a healthy sign.'

"Maybe. But living in the middle of it isn't so great!"

"What are you going to do?" It was a matter-of-fact question. She asked it as though she were sure I'd have an answer, but I didn't share her optimism. I got up from the chair and swung a leg over the deck rail, straddling it as I looked at the river.

"The main thing is Georgie. The rest of us can take care of ourselves, but he's too little. I don't know what I *will* do, but I know what I won't do. I won't let Dad bully him any more."

She nodded. "There are lots of pieces to sort out, Neal. Georgie's problem is one piece. The family relationships are another, and your own life apart from your folks is another. The music fits in there, and it's very important."

"Yes, I know about all those pieces. The trouble is that I've been trying to keep them separate from one another all this time, and it won't work. Everything is connected, whether I like it or not. Changing one piece means changing all the pieces."

"Bravo!" she said softly. She smiled, but she had tears in her eyes, too. "You're much wiser than I was at your age. The problem is, you learn more than you want to when bad things happen. I found that out when I was about twice your age."

"What happened?"

She hesitated a moment, but then seemed to make up her mind. "My husband became ill. He had a rare, degenerative disease that eventually affected his mind as well as his body. He died after being sick a long, long time. I had to make some hard choices then like the ones you're having to make now. You are right—the pieces go together."

I wondered what to say. Suddenly I could see why she understood things so well. It was plain that Mrs. T. still felt sad about what had happened to her husband, even after all this time. If that was what had made her wise, it seemed hardly worth the pain.

"Well," I said after a while, "maybe the day will come when I'll be glad for what I'm learning from all this, but right now I'd gladly trade it for a large dose of innocence."

"What do you expect when you go home this evening?" she asked.

I realized as soon as she asked the question that I'd been doing everything I could to keep from thinking about that.

"Lots of silence. Dad shut up in the study if he's home. Mom worrying herself to a frazzle, trying to figure out what to do. She'd already planned to ask Dad about getting psychiatric help for Georgie, but then these rumors popped up. I don't know what she's done." I sighed again. "It's tough for her. She feels responsible for finding a way out of the mess, but she has to go against Dad to do it. I think she's scared."

"I'm glad you understand that," Mrs. T. said. "Who does she talk to?"

"Nobody. If she ever told anyone here what was really going on, she'd feel like a fink. She's probably said more about it to me than to anyone else, but I don't like it very much."

"Do you think she'd talk to me?"

I felt a twinge of guilt. "I don't know. Mom's proud. She'd hate it if she knew how much you know about us."

"I understand." She got up and began to pace the deck. The river breeze blew her hair and whipped the caftan about her body. "Well, then, we'll just have to leave things as they are for the time being. You know I'll help in whatever way I can. Perhaps in a day or two you'll get an idea of what that help should be."

"Thanks," I said. I swung my leg back to the deck and looked at my watch. "I believe I can stand to go home now I owe you for a lesson—the one you canceled."

"I expect I'll get paid back one of these days," she said gently. "Many times over."

Mom came out on the porch to meet me when I crossed the street to our house.

"There you are," she said. "I was worried."

"Didn't Georgie tell you where I was?"

"Yes. I wasn't worried about *where* you were—only about whether you'd bother to come home."

I came up on the porch. "Why not? This is where I live."

"Well, after what happened this morning, I wasn't sure you'd think this place was worth coming home to."

"Is Dad raving?"

"No. He seems to have put this morning out of his mind completely."

"Well," I said, "am I supposed to pretend it didn't happen, too?"

"*I* don't know!" She sounded exasperated. "Just be yourself."

I went past her into the hallway and up the stairs. *Be yourself.* What would it be like to be myself here, not to have to weigh consequences of words and acts all the time? As it was, we had each developed our own personal censor, even Aileen, who was better than the rest of us at saying what she thought.

I flopped backward on the rumpled bed, thinking about what had forced us into hiding.

We just didn't fit Dad's idea of what a minister's family ought to be. None of us. Mom tried to conform, but she was losing heart. As for the rest of us, we were a constant embarrassment to him. Even when we did our best, he didn't expect it to last. Maybe he'd be happy if he could be rid of us and start over with a fresh bunch—turn us in for new models programmed from the beginning to Act Right.

I imagined the scene as he went into an electronics store and asked for a robot wife and three kids of assorted sizes and ages. He'd get a trade-in allowance on us according to how old we were and how used or how useful. The new family would smile a lot and never talk back. Maybe he'd keep them in boxes except when he needed them grouped around him to look like the perfect family.

But even while I grinned at my own invention, something dark began rising inside me, starting in the pit of my stomach and spreading out to my arms and fingers, my toes, my head.

It was Georgie's fear—being replaced by someone more acceptable.

I lay there in a cold sweat, heart pounding, and let myself go down into that darkness where Georgie must live all the time. It was terrifying. I fought against the power of the feeling, but the fear of being overwhelmed became too much for me. I rolled over and sat up, sure that if I waited another few seconds it would be too late to escape. For a long time I just sat on the edge of the bed, breathing hard and staring at the floor. I couldn't shake off the strangeness.

When I went down to dinner I felt as though I weren't really inside myself any more, that the body making its way to the dining room belonged to someone else. When we were all seated around the table, it seemed that I was in a *picture* of us seated around the table. Nobody said anything. No one looked anyone else in the eye.

"Let's bow our heads for grace," Dad intoned. I stared down at my plate gleaming under the light. The words of the blessing were as empty and smooth as its surface.

"I'm on the track of those rumors," Dad said immediately after the amen. We passed the food and served ourselves, and no one asked him any questions. Maybe this is the way he has always wanted us to be—a set of ears for his words to fall upon. No mouths to answer back. I imagined us like that, with the lower parts of our faces sealed over and blank. I watched his hands, one on each side of his plate, as the fingers splayed outward and pressed against the white tablecloth.

"Yes," he continued, as though someone had commented. "I believe I'll know very soon who started this mess. I've been making inquiries."

The silence deepened. Georgie's head bent over his plate. He had his left hand in his lap, trying hard to mind his manners the way he'd been taught. He struggled to chase down a couple of stray peas with his fork, concentrating mightily on it. Whatever was being said had nothing to do with him. For the second time that day I wished I were seven years old again.

"Well," Dad said, "isn't anyone interested?"

"I think it might be just as well to let the matter drop," Mom said.

"Are you serious? Until this is cleared up once and for all, I'll have no peace." He swung around toward me. "Today Mr. Thompson looked at me as though I'd lost my mind. I felt— under the circumstances—that the less I said the better. Why provide grist for the mill?"

What was I supposed to say to that? I was on Mr. Thompson's side.

"You're imagining things, Richard," Mom said. "He didn't look at you strangely until you—"

She stopped.

"Until I what?"

Silence grew under his glare. Her distress was plain. She did not know what to do.

"Until you made an ass of yourself!" I shouted, stunned at my own recklessness.

Everyone gasped. For one glorious instant I felt that I'd snatched the cloth and dishes from under everyone's nose, the way I'd always dreamed of doing. But reality quickly moved in.

"How dare you!" he rasped, rising from his seat. "Leave this table immediately!"

I got up from the table and went out quickly, before anyone could see the tears starting. I raced out of the house, took the five steps in a single leap, and hit the ground running. If he called my name again, I didn't want to be close enough to hear it.

CHAPTER 18

I ran until I had a stitch in my right side and then walked, pressing my hand against the spot just under my ribs. Breathing hurt, but it was all so mixed with anger and sadness I couldn't tell which was the worse pain. I didn't have any idea where I was heading, except I wanted to get as far away from home as possible. Sure, I'd have to go back sooner or later, mostly because of Georgie, but I had to regroup. In the meantime Dad would be dreaming up my punishment. What form would it take? How much could I resist? Being obedient all these years had taken its toll. I haven't had much practice rebelling; I seem to be pretty clumsy at it.

The after-dinner porch sitters weren't out yet, and the empty street gave the illusion that the whole town was deserted. In a nightmare I had when I was a kid everyone in the whole town suddenly disappeared but me . . . and some evil thing that lurked in dark doorways. The terror of the nightmare stayed with me for years—I used to dread that it would actually happen. But now I couldn't help thinking that being the only person in town might solve a lot of problems. There'd be no one left to run away from, to hide from, to blame, to worry about, or to show off for. I might even become Real.

I dug in my jeans pocket and found two quarters, enough for a cold drink. Once I had the drink in hand, I'd go down to the pier back of Bailey's store and stay there until after dark. Maybe by that time I'd know what to do next.

I cut across the street to Bailey's, distracted by thirst and by the scene I'd left behind. That's probably why I didn't notice until too late the lone figure sitting on a pile of crates in front of the store.

Pete Cauthin.

"Where you goin'?" he said, holding a Pepsi can loosely in one large hand. Somehow he manages to look tough even when he's sitting still.

"To get a drink." I started into the store.

"Hold on a minute." He signaled with a jerk of his head that I should come back and help finish the conversation he'd started.

Reluctantly I backed away from the entrance, but I stayed near the front. If he tore into me I wanted it to be where someone else could witness the fact.

"I'm meetin' Aileen up the street in thirty minutes. We're goin to the movie in Wayside."

"Fine," I said stiffly.

"You think I'm a bum because I don't go to the house to pick her up like boyfriends are supposed to?"

I shrugged. "It's none of my business."

He stood up. It was all I could do not to take a quick step backward. "You're right, it's not. But I just wanted you to know I don't do it only because your preacher pa would give her a hard time. She can't stand up to him but just so much without gettin' hurt. I'm not afraid of him—I could beat him to a pulp. But it wouldn't do her any good."

He was right, of course. My mind worked, trying to gauge his tone, to figure why he was telling me this. He didn't seem to be particularly bothered that I wasn't talking.

"You know, you kinda surprised me yesterday," he went on. "I thought you'd try to get out of ISS. You could've, you know. You could've told 'em I started it and they'd've believed you."

"Why would I have done that?" I asked. "Once it got started, I'd have killed you gladly."

"You like to've done it, too," he commented, putting his hand up to the scabbed-over cut at the corner of his mouth. "Anyhow, you could've got out of it. A word from your dad would've got you off."

"It never crossed his mind to get me off," I said bitterly. "He thought I deserved to be punished."

Pete looked surprised. "Is that the truth? I'd've thought he'd rather beat you up in the privacy of your home than to let it get out that his precious boy was being punished by the principal."

"Look, Pete, lay off. I'm not bothering you and I don't want to start something—"

"It's all right," he said, gesturing with the hand that held the drink. "Now you've done it you can see sinnin' ain't as bad as it's cracked up to be."

I couldn't understand what he was getting at or his amiable manner. What did he want from me?

"What's the matter?" he asked. There was an edge to his voice.

"I don't know," I mumbled. "I'm just not good at quick changes."

"You sure aren't!" he said with mild disgust. "You know, what made me maddest yesterday was that you offered to settle for the boat. It was such a goody-goody thing to do—something to make *me* look bad if I took you up on it. That's the thing about you I've never liked—how you always manage to stay on the right side of the rules, always do what makes you look good. Up till now I've never seen you risk gettin' in trouble. But now maybe there's hope for you—"

"What's the good of it? Why make everyone mad at you? What does it get you?" I shouted, surprised at my own heat.

"Sometimes it gets you fun!" he yelled back. "Sometimes it gets you love! Sometimes it gets you excitement! It might get you some bad things, too, but bein' good all the time just ain't real— it ain't natural!"

I was stunned. The words he spoke seemed to freeze in the air above us in large imposing letters.

"Aw, hell!" he said, shifting abruptly. He hurled his drink can. It clanked and clattered on the pavement an incredible distance away, then with his long stride he followed the sound in the direction of his car. I stood there for several seconds after he left.

After that unnerving encounter Mr. Bailey's store was like a warm, welcoming hand with its familiar smells—the bread shelf, the meat cabinet, the fertilizer in the side room. I was the only customer. In fact, for a minute I wondered whether anyone was in the store besides me, but Mr. Bailey came out of the little office in the back when I opened the refrigerated cabinet to take out a drink.

"Well, how do, Neal! What're you doing here this time of day?"

"I've been running," I said, hoping I looked normal even though I didn't feel that way. I handed him the money and turned to go out.

"Are you in a big hurry?" he asked. "If you're not, I'd like to talk to you."

My heart began to pound, from what I could not say. "O.K. I have a little while."

"Come on back here in the office so we won't be interrupted if somebody comes in."

I opened the drink and followed him into the crowded little room. It was hardly big enough to turn around in because of Mr. Bailey's rolltop desk, which was half-submerged under a pile of papers. The place smelled of aged paper and cardboard.

"You sit there." He indicated a chair with leather as wrinkled and cracked as an old man's skin. He sat down behind the desk, looking at me with such concern that I became more uneasy than ever. I took a quick swallow of the drink.

"What is it?" I asked.

'Well, I don't rightly know. I thought you could shed some ight on the subject for me " he said, rubbing one hand over his hair.

I waited, mystified.

"You remember your little brother came in here one day, and he and I made an arrangement that he'd buy some things and pay me back on time. I'll admit that at first I tried to discourage it—I didn't want every little boy and girl in Gideon in here askin' for credit, you understand!" He chuckled a little, but when I didn't respond he became serious again. "Anyhow, he begged so hard I finally agreed. When I suggested he get your dad to advance him the money, he got all upset. He told me he couldn't ask your dad for anything right now, because things weren't so good."

I sat forward in the chair. "What did he say?"

"Well, he got to stuttering. He could hardly get the words out, but best I can remember, he said something like, 'I think he's in trouble. I think maybe he might lose his job.' I'll admit that kind of shocked me. When I tried to ask him some questions, he got more and more nervous. He mumbled something about his dad not feeling very well and then another time said he didn't act like himself. Nothing earth-shaking, so far as that goes, except you don't usually hear that sort of thing from seven-year-olds."

"Oh, no!" I groaned. "I can't believe he'd do that!"

"I didn't know what to think," said Mr. Bailey. "I don't like to go tending to somebody else's business, so I just let it go. I sort of put it to what you said that day you came in here—an overactive imagination. But then—"

"Then what?"

"This morning Hal Lutz came in here telling that Mr. Sloan was out looking for whoever it was started the tales about him. The more he talked, the more I realized it sounded like the things Georgie said here in this store. I never repeated what he told me, but Jolene Milbanks was working in here that day, and I don't know what she heard—or what she might've said to somebody else."

I got up and went to the door of the office, then came back. "Mr. Bailey, that's awful!"

"I've been in a bind to know what to do," he said. "Sooner or later your dad would find out where it started. I was thinking maybe I should sort of head him off—you know, try to explain the whole thing so he'd realize the little fellow didn't mean any harm. I think he just began telling a little story and it swelled up and got away from him."

I tossed the empty drink can into the wastebasket and sat down in the chair again, my head in my hands. Some of the missing pieces had begun to fall into place. No wonder Georgie was so interested in what Dad would do when he found the culprit! I thought about all the things Georgie had told that Mom and Dad labeled "Lies." But by the time he told them, he was convinced they were true. No one in the family hated lies more than Georgie did. What was making him sick was having to live in the middle of a Great Lie as though nothing were wrong.

I looked up at Mr. Bailey's worried face. "What did he buy that day?" I asked.

He scratched his chin, thinking. "I might not remember all of it, but I do remember it was things like cans of soup, a box of crackers, some raisins. Stuff like that. You'd expect a little fellow to buy ice cream and bubble gum, but he didn't."

"Did he say why he wanted it?"

"No. I teased him a bit—I asked him if he was fixing up a bomb shelter."

Someone came into the store just then, and Mr. Bailey excused himself to go wait on the customer. I went on sitting in the chair, trying to think what to do. The whole crazy mess was a time bomb. There was no telling what Dad would do when he found out, but how could any of us bury the secret deep enough to prevent an explosion? If only Georgie could go away for a while— maybe to visit Gran Rogers. I dismissed that idea as soon as it popped into my head, though. Gran has always treated Georgie like an unlucky accident.

I went out into the store and over to the meat counter, where Mr. Bailey was weighing ground beef. "I have to go now," I said.

"Wait a second—let me wrap this up. There's one more thing I need to tell you."

I waited by the door, staring out of the windows into the dusky street. It was after eight o'clock. The sun had gone down, and the air had become twilight blue. What could I do to save Georgie from Dad's wrath? I'd never felt more helpless.

"The thing I wanted to tell you," Mr. Bailey said suddenly at my elbow, "was that a minute or two before you got here, I called up your dad. I told him I had an idea where the stories came from, and that they were the result of somebody misunderstanding and embroidering on what the little fellow said. I didn't get any further with my explanation, though, because your dad got so upset he hung up and didn't let me finish—"

All the blood in my heart was suddenly in my feet.

"Oh, for God's sake—why didn't you tell me that first!" I yelled. I flung myself out the door and raced down the street toward home, only this time it was fear and not anger that drove me. The wind blew up from the river and pushed against me, an added hindrance. I was in a nightmare and could not move fast enough.

As I neared our house, I thought I heard someone crying, but when I slowed to listen I decided I was mistaken. The wind intensified, blowing through the tall oaks and maples that lined the street, setting up a continuous loud whisper in the leaves.

Not until I was on the porch did I hear through the open door the sound of Georgie sobbing. Over the sobbing Dad's voice rose and fell, heated and quietly violent. The hair rose on the back of my neck. I slipped inside and closed the door behind me, then, sweating and still trying to catch my breath, I went along the hall to the living room.

It was a scene straight out of the Inquisition. Dad's back was turned so he didn't see me. Mom stood by the Morris chair, holding on to it for dear life, her terrified eyes on his face. Georgie was in the middle of the room, his thin legs planted far apart, his head bent under the wash of words.

"I've had it with you, George!" The words sizzled like spit on hot metal. "It's one thing to tell lies here at home—that's bad enough, God knows—but when you spread them all over town—"

"But I didn't!" Georgie wailed weakly. "I didn't!'"

"Hey, what is this?" I interrupted.

Dad whirled, startled. "It's none of your concern! Go to your room—I'll attend to you later!"

I came on in, feeling like the guy in the bull ring whose job is to wave the red cape. "Whose concern is it?" I said, as calmly as I could.

"Get out!"

Georgie's trembling legs stuck out from his short pants. He looked so weak and white I thought of a mouse in a python's cage, except there the mice don't usually know enough to be scared.

"It seems to me," I said carefully, "that maybe you're too upset now to be fair."

"He's sick!" Dad shouted. He, too, was shaking. "His mind is sick! He needs to be put away somewhere—he's dangerous!"

"Richard, don't say that in front of him!" Tears coursed down Mom's cheeks. She seemed chained to the spot.

I went over and put my arm around Georgie's nothing little shoulders. His whole body quaked. "Dad, he's just a little guy—"

My eyes were on a level with his. What I saw in them made me want to bolt and run, but I didn't. I wasn't going anywhere without Georgie.

"I told you I'd find out, and I have. There he is, my own son, spreading lies about me! Ruining my life, my position. No *normal* child would ever think of doing such a thing—"

Georgie was transfixed, impaled on Dad's anger. He tried to speak, but no sound came.

"You're mistaken, Dad." I don't know how I managed to keep my voice even. "You didn't wait to hear the rest of Mr. Bailey's explanation. I'm taking Georgie upstairs. When you calm down some, maybe we can talk about it."

I turned Georgie to lead him out of the room. The next instant Dad's hand grasped my shoulder from behind.

"Young man, *I'll* say when he can leave the room! I'm in charge here!"

"Then act like it!" I shouted.

His hand came up and struck me across the face. Mom screamed. In the lightning shock of it I could have killed him on the spot. Holding Georgie against me, I practically dragged him from the room. If Dad laid a hand on me again I knew I'd beat the daylights out of him. Maybe he knew it too, because he didn't try to stop me.

"Come on, fella," I said, pulling Georgie up the stairs. We bumped against each other on the way. I heard Mom's footsteps behind us, and I turned. "Leave us alone!" I shouted at her. "Just keep that creep from following us!"

We went into Georgie's room, and I locked the door, then we sat on the bed. I held him until the jerking and trembling calmed some. The side of my face flamed. I thought I could feel the marks of each separate finger of Dad's hand.

When I tried to think what to do next, the thoughts skittered away like little black bugs. I was scared. I had been to the edge of a dark pit and looked in. Now my mind didn't want to believe or remember what it had seen. In a moment Georgie slumped. I leaned down and looked in his face. His eyes were closing.

"You want to sleep in my room tonight?" I asked.

He shook his head dumbly. Maybe he only felt safe here in this room with his own things. I looked around. It was really tiny—almost a closet. It was, in fact, a storage room before he was born, a kind of closed-off space at the back of the hall. It struck me all of a sudden how when he came along we had made as little room for him as possible. Like four people spread out comfortably on a bench, we were unwilling to move over. Maybe that's why he's always been so small—he must have known he'd have to squeeze into whatever space he could find.

His pajamas were folded neatly beside his pillow, something

he'd done so Mom would be pleased with him. I'd never had to go to such lengths to get her approval. In fact, I couldn't remember being worried very much about what she thought of me one way or the other.

"Let's put on your pj's," I said. "I'll stay here with you. I won't let him get to you."

He was limp and unresponsive as I took off his clothes and put on the pajamas. I pulled back the covers and tucked him in. His eyes closed. He was like a dead person.

"Georgie," I said close to his ear. "Nobody's going to hurt you."

Nothing. Not a flicker of an eyelid or a twitch of a muscle. I had never seen anyone so still. It was as though what had happened had burned his brain blank.

CHAPTER 19

I stayed in his room for a long time, sitting on the rug beside his bed. For a while I expected Dad to bang on the door and yell to be let in, but when it didn't happen I relaxed some. I kept seeing Mom crying while she watched Dad haul Georgie over the coals. As much as she hated it, she seemed powerless to act against him. How must Georgie have felt when she didn't defend him? What if I hadn't come back when I did?

He lay in exactly the position he had fallen asleep, his head turned on the pillow, his mouth slightly open. Without his glasses he looked like one of those fragile angel carvings you see on old tombstones.

What would become of him? I never again wanted to see him and Dad in the same room together, but what could I do about it? Morning would come and another day. If we Sloans followed our pattern, we'd go along as though nothing out of the ordinary had happened. No one would speak of it.

That thought and the rage it ignited in me brought me to my feet. Georgie was so sound asleep he didn't hear me get up and go out. From the top of the stairs I heard voices murmuring in the kitchen. I couldn't give myself time to think over what I was about to do, or I wouldn't be able to do it.

They sat close together at the kitchen table, and from the looks of things they had both been crying. When they saw me, they looked surprised and scared. I thought it strange that they should be afraid of me.

"Hello, Neal," Mom said. "Come sit with us."

I shook my head. I didn't want to be anywhere near them.

All life had gone out of Dad. He looked at me with dull eyes. "I'm sorry, Neal," he said hoarsely.

I didn't feel anything. It was weird. "What're you going to do?" I asked.

They glanced at each other, then Mom spoke. "We're going to get help."

I should be glad, I thought. I should leap up and click my heels together. But I didn't feel anything.

"It's like a prophecy come true," Dad said in a strange, toneless voice. "This is a troubled family. I don't know how it happened. How *did* it happen? We're healthy, normal people . . ."

Mom touched his hand and he stopped talking. "I have to go up to check on Georgie," she said. "I want to be sure he's all right."

"Don't go near him," I said harshly. "He's sleeping, and if he wakes up and sees you there's no telling what he'll do!"

"Neal, I . . ." She began to cry again, putting up her hands to hide her face.

"I don't want to hear it!" My voice rose. "He's just a little guy. You're his parents, the people he ought to be able to count on for love and protection, and you aren't worth shit to him!"

They sat there and took it, and somehow that enraged me even more. "Tomorrow," I said, "you two get over to the clinic in Hatboro. I'm not leaving Georgie alone with either of you, not even if I have to handcuff us together."

Mom wiped her eyes and stood up. "All right, Neal. I won't bother Georgie tonight if you're sure he's all right. But you need to remember that we *are* your parents, and you can't make the decisions that have to be made. Your father and I have talked about the counseling, and we've agreed that's what must be done. Until tomorrow that's the best we can do."

I was feeling mean. "How'd she talk you into it?" I asked Dad, and braced myself for a flood of excuses and criticism.

"She didn't have to talk me into it," he said in a low voice, looking away. His face was heavy with sadness. I began to feel uneasy. Awful as he was the other way, at least I knew what to expect.

"I'm leaving the door to my room open so I can listen for Georgie," I said. "Tomorrow morning you'd better be ready to do some apologizing and let him know things are going to be different. I just hope it's not too late."

I left them sitting there. I'd said what I wanted to say, but I felt rotten all the same. Upstairs again I sat on the edge of my bed in the darkness. I intended to stay awake until Aileen came home, so I could let her know what had happened. Somehow, though, I didn't make it. I went to sleep with my clothes on.

I woke up suddenly, and it was dark, the sort of cottony gray dark of early morning. Outside, a few birds chirped, but they weren't really into it, so I knew it was nowhere near time to get up. I lay very still for a few seconds, trying to remember what had awakened me. There wasn't a sound from within the house, not even so much as a creaking board. I thought I could hear my own blood rushing.

Then slowly consciousness returned, and along with it a lot of feelings I'd as soon forget.

Georgie.

It was supposed to be the beginning of a new era for the Richard Sloan household. But even as I lay there I didn't believe things were going to be different. In the light of day Dad would decide things weren't so serious after all. He and Mom would put off seeing the psychiatrist in Hatboro. There'd be lots of dodging—nobody talking about what had happened or being straight with each other. I turned over and covered my head with the bedspread, determined not to think about it any more.

Problem is, I can't turn my brain off just by wishing it. I must've relived that scene with Dad half a dozen times. The ending was always Georgie's little white face lying on the pillow. It took all my will power not to get up and go to his room just to be sure he was all right, but I knew that was stupid. I'd only wake him up and get him frightened again.

The room grew steadily lighter. The alarm clock said six. I didn't have to get up for another thirty minutes, but I was too fidgety to stay put. I got up, showered, changed into fresh clothes, and went downstairs. I could hear the slap of Mom's floppy bedroom slippers on the kitchen tile.

"H'lo," I mumbled.

"For goodness' sakes—what are you doing up so early?" she exclaimed, wiping one damp hand on her flowered housecoat. "I thought I wouldn't be able to rouse you even at the regular time."

"I couldn't sleep." I came on into the kitchen.

"I'm not surprised." Her eyes were dark and sad. "Here—as long as you're here you can mix the orange juice."

We worked in silence for a few minutes; she gave the orders and I carried them out. It was kind of nice, but I was aware of all the things we weren't saying. They were a wall between us. I heard the alarm clock go off in the downstairs bedroom and knew that Dad would be getting up. Pretty soon we'd all be sitting down to breakfast together. . . .

"What's the plan?" I asked. "Or is it any of my business?"

She was making biscuits, and she thumped and kneaded the dough with great concentration. At last she said, "I'm going to call Dr. Koch as soon as his office opens. I'll ask for a referral to the clinic in Hatboro and let him know it's an emergency. Perhaps we'll be able to go there today."

"What about Georgie?"

"I don't know. It depends upon how he is this morning. He may not want you out of his sight. If that's the case, I'll make arrangements for you to miss school today."

"It looks as though Dad is leaving you to make all the decisions."

"Why not? I've been thinking about it longer. It doesn't matter, so long as something is done."

She glanced at the clock as she put the biscuits into the oven a few minutes later. "Neal, would you go make sure that Aileen is up, and check on Georgie? Breakfast should be ready in another ten minutes."

I took the steps two at a time. Aileen's door was open and the noise of the shower came from the bathroom, so I didn't bother to yell at her. Georgie's door was still shut. I tapped cautiously with one fingernail, then turned the knob and went in.

He wasn't there. The bed was made, and his pajamas were neatly folded. His schoolbooks were piled on the desk. Nothing was out of place.

"Georgie?"

I felt silly saying it, and I felt silly looking in his closet, too, but I wanted him to be there. He wasn't.

I backed out of the room and closed the door, feeling tightness in my chest. I went to Aileen's room and peered in, just on the chance he had gone in there to wait for her, but there was no sign of him.

The shower stopped. I knocked on the bathroom door. In a moment Aileen stuck her towel-wrapped head out.

"What do you want?" she said irritably. "Can't you use the downstairs bathroom?"

"I think Georgie's gone," I said.

She looked at me uncomprehendingly. "What do you mean?"

"I mean he's not in his room."

"Well, have you looked anywhere else in the house? How about *your* room?" She didn't seem to be particularly alarmed, just annoyed. "Look, I can't do a thing about it until I get my clothes on. Go look for him. He's bound to be around here somewhere." She shut the door firmly, and the lock clicked.

Maybe she was right. Since she hadn't been here for the furor, she wasn't as likely to get upset. I went to my room, hoping that when I opened the door I'd see him over at my desk by the window, waiting for me in his patient way. I hoped it so hard that for about one-tenth of a second I really did see him there, but my imagination is only good for flashes. My room was as empty as his, but messier.

I told myself not to panic before being sure. Downstairs again, I looked out the glass side panes of the front door, thinking he might be sitting on the front porch for some reason. It was just wishful thinking. One by one I went through all the downstairs rooms except the bathroom, where Dad was shaving. Then I went back to the kitchen.

"Mom," I said, "I think Georgie's gone."

She turned white. "Neal, don't tease about things like that!"

"I'm not teasing. I can't find him. His bed's made up—"

She flew past me and up the stairs. I followed more slowly. Aileen was just coming out of her room.

"Haven't you found him yet?" she asked. Mom didn't answer, just tore into his room and began looking under things and behind furniture.

"Aw, Mom—he wouldn't hide like that!" I said. "And I've already looked everywhere in the house. He's not here."

"You told me you'd listen for him!" she said angrily. "I didn't come up here last night because you said you'd—"

"Now don't go blaming *me*!" I yelled. "Just because—"

"Say, what *is* this!" Aileen stepped between us. "You two are acting like you've lost your marbles. Maybe Georgie's in the backyard or something. Why all the panic?'

"And where were you last night that you didn't hear?" Mom asked.

Aileen got very quiet, but Mom didn't pursue the matter—her mind was on more important things.

"Where could he be?" she pleaded, turning to me with her palms open to hold any answer she could get. "And how long has he been gone? When did you last see him?"

"When I came down to talk to you and Dad last night. Afterward I went to my room and went to sleep. I slept like a rock until—"

And then something in my brain clicked.

"Hey, maybe that's what woke me up this morning—the front door opening! He must have gotten up early to go out. Maybe he went to the landing."

"Oh, I hope so! Please, Neal—run and see if he's there."

"What if he's not?"

"Then get back here as quickly as you can. We have to start looking. He may—" She couldn't go on. Fear made her face taut.

"I'm going now," I said. "Tell Aileen what's up. I'll be back soon."

Please let him be with Captain, I thought as I raced toward the landing. If he's there I'll fix it somehow so he can stay there as long as he needs to. Just let him be there.

I was out of breath when I reached the landing, and I leaned against a tree to rest. No one was out that early in the morning. The gulls wheeled and dived, filling the quiet air with their noisy squawking. Any other day I would have been perfectly content to sit down by the tree and watch them, but not now.

I took the roundabout path that Georgie had showed me on Sunday and came up beside Captain's houseboat in the little inlet. The boat hardly moved in the smooth water. A large gull had made himself comfortable on the cabin top and stared out toward the sound like an ancient admiral. At the water's edge I cupped my hands around my mouth and yelled.

"Captain! Captain Perry!"

I waited for what seemed like a long time, then called again. At last the cabin door opened and Captain's round, ruddy face poked out. I waved.

"Captain, it's me—Neal Sloan! I'm looking for Georgie. Have you seen him?"

He came out on the deck, shading his eyes to see me better. I yelled again. "Georgie left and didn't tell anyone where he was going! Do you know where he might be?"

My voice cracked, and I knew I was about to bawl. I swallowed hard to keep it down. This was no time for me to start acting like a baby.

Captain called back something unintelligible, shaking his head. He signaled that he was going to put down the plank and that I should wait. I stood first on one foot, then on the other, fighting back the tears.

The plank slid into the water at my feet, and I climbed it, remembering how Georgie had scampered so lightly along it the day we came together. Captain reached for my arm and steadied me as I climbed over the rail, then, looking me in the eye, he didn't let go.

I really did cry then. I couldn't talk or anything. I thought my insides were going to come up. Captain led me to a crate and made me sit down. At some point he handed me a fishy-smelling handkerchief. I used it to wipe my face, trying to stop the flow, but I couldn't.

"O-'ay," he said at last, giving me a heavy-handed pat on the shoulder. " 'es yook foh Joge, now."

When I looked up and saw the pain and worry in his eyes, some giant hand turned off whatever had broken loose inside me. I quit crying. He went over the rail and down the plank like a true sailor, and I stumbled along after him.

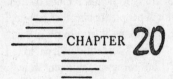

CHAPTER 20

Because of Captain's age and shorter legs, it took longer for the two of us to cover the distance between the landing and our house than it had taken me by myself. On the way he asked many questions: when had I last seen Georgie? Did he seem scared or worried? I debated keeping our family secrets, but then decided to hell with it—Captain was Georgie's best friend. He ought to know what we were up against, so I told him what had happened the night before. He did not appear to be angry, only sad.

"If I'd had any sense I would've stayed in the room with him all night," I said. "But he was so wiped out. He looked like he wouldn't move for hours."

" 'ont wo'y," Captain said, giving me a pat on the arm. "Mebbe Joge 'es hidin'."

When we reached the house at last, Mom, Dad, and Aileen were waiting for us on the porch. Aileen ran down the steps to meet us.

"He wasn't there, was he?" she said. "Oh. Neal, I could kill myself for not being here last night!"

"Well, that's all over and done with," I said. "Do you think Pete would help us look?"

"I'm sure of it." She gave me a grateful look. "I'll go call him right now. He probably hasn't left for school yet."

"Call Mrs. Talbot, too," I said. "I think . . . we're going to need all the help we can get."

We made an odd group gathered there on the porch—Captain,

Mom, Dad, and I. Captain was ill at ease, but I wasn't sure whether it was because he couldn't talk plainly or because being on land makes him generally uncomfortable. Dad was . . . well, different. He wasn't putting on at all. Now he just seemed baffled.

"I don't know that we need a lot of people looking for Georgie," he said. "Gideon's not that big. I think we'll find him quickly."

"Well, *I'm* not sure," I said. "There's something I have to tell you. I promised him I wouldn't, but things are different now."

Aileen came back out just then and announced that both Pete and Mrs. T. were on their way. She listened as I told them about what Georgie believed about us—that we were False people who had replaced his real family.

"For a while he was convinced that every one of us was some sort of spy, because he couldn't believe that a real family would treat him so badly. Then he decided that maybe I wasn't False yet. His great fear was that sooner or later *he* was going to be replaced, too. He was always on the alert for a sign that the False people were closing in on him. I guess what happened last night was it. Maybe he thought if he didn't leave before morning, he'd never get another chance. I don't think we're going to find him behind a stump or under a bush. I believe he had a plan."

Mom and Dad scarcely moved during my recital. Their faces were full of shock. "It's so strange!" Mom breathed. "He's so little. How could he imagine something so complicated and . . . and horrible?"

"I guess his imagination is more active than most kids', and what was going on here just fed into it. We haven't been too wonderful to him, you know."

"I never intended—" Dad began, but he couldn't finish. He looked down, blinking back tears. I wished Georgie could see him. He would know that Dad was Real, after all.

"You say Georgie had a plan?" Mom asked. "What was it?"

"I don't know. He never told me, and I didn't ask because I didn't really think he'd go that far."

Mrs. T. came running across the street just then, dressed in jeans and hiking boots, as though she meant business. There was a little flurry as she shook hands with Captain and Dad, gave Mom a quick hug, and ticked off a list of people we should notify, including Chief Partridge, Gideon's only policeman. Nobody argued. Within a few minutes we had all decided where to look and when to report back.

Captain and I confined our searching to the waterfront. He borrowed a boat, and we cruised slowly up and down the river, checking out all Georgie's favorite places along the shore. He steered while I used his binoculars to scan the shoreline. Captain thought Georgie might have tried hiding under some of the clay bluffs at the upper end of town. If that was the case, he couldn't be seen by anyone on land.

We made the trip up and back. Captain's face became more and more grim.

"Do you think he might have taken a boat to cross the river?" I asked.

He shook his head. "Joge don't y'ike mo'h bo'h."

It was true. Georgie didn't like machines, particularly noisy ones like boat motors. "Well, then, what do we do now?"

Captain looked around at the wide expanse of water. The breeze had come up, and the surface was becoming choppy. "Wo' mo' 'ime," he said, turning the boat and heading back the way we had just come. It seemed to me that his speech was becoming more distinct the longer we were together.

It was on the way back that I saw the skiff adrift a little to port. I couldn't imagine why I hadn't seen it the first time around, but I guess we'd been concentrating so hard on the shoreline we just hadn't looked out on the river.

Captain and I caught sight of it at the same time. Without a word he headed toward it. When we pulled alongside I think I hoped Georgie would be lying flat on the bottom trying to stay out of sight, but of course he wasn't. One oar lay as though it had been thrown there haphazardly. Captain studied it for a moment and checked the mooring line.

"Untie'," he said, holding up the rope to show me that it wasn't frazzled like one that wears and breaks.

"You know whose boat it is?" I asked.

He nodded. "It b'ong Bi' B'oo. It 'tay at t' yandin'."

"Did . . . does Georgie know it's there?"

He hesitated a moment before answering. Then he told me that Georgie often sat in the boat and pretended to be rowing it while it was tied to the pier. Bill Blue didn't use the boat any more and had been thinking about selling it.

"You're sure that's the boat?"

He pointed to the name Bonny Blue on the side. "Joge yike it. He wan' buy it."

"Captain, you don't think Georgie would untie the boat and try to go somewhere in it by himself, do you?"

He frowned. "He nev' di' befo'."

"There's only one oar," I said. "If he started out with two—"

Captain didn't say anything. He fastened the skiff to our boat and we headed back to the landing with the throttle open. The boat spanked the waves rhythmically, and the skiff danced like a wild thing in our wake. Somehow I didn't want to look down into the water any more. I kept my eyes straight ahead, looking at distant buoy markers.

I hated myself.

If I'd stayed with him during the night, it wouldn't have happened. Or if I hadn't stormed out of the house at dinnertime, or if I'd pushed Mom not to waste time getting the help that Georgie—all of us—needed. I knew now that he'd never come home on his own. I feared that in his terror he'd do something really dangerous. We might not be able to get to him in time.

I began to feel sick at my stomach. I propped my elbows on my knees and held my head in my hands, trying to think back to our conversations. Maybe he'd said something that would give a clue about where to look for him. It was no use, though—there was nothing to go on except Mr. Bailey's information that Georgie had bought food supplies and not junk with his five-dollar credit.

Mr. Bailey had teased him about fixing up a bomb shelter. So . . . had he found a hiding place ahead of time, or had he set out with his supplies this morning in the skiff to find one across the river?

We pulled into the landing. Captain quickly moored the larger boat, giving me instructions about where the skiff should be tied.

"We 'ave t'go teh Chee Po'trij," he said gravely. "He w'an see bo'."

"You don't really believe Georgie was in that boat, do you, Captain?"

He didn't try to hide his worry. "Nee', ah don' no'."

We left the landing and hurried up the street to our house. It had been taken over by church members and neighbors manning the telephone and bringing in food. That's what people do here when there's trouble or sickness—they go into a cooking spasm. Hell! I thought. Who could eat?

Maybe you've seen on television what happens when kids disappear, at least in towns like Gideon where practically every hair of every person's head is numbered. While the rest of us were looking, Mrs. T. had notified the school and everyone else she could think of who might have a clue. The highway patrol and the county sheriff's department had been alerted in case Georgie was spotted somewhere out of town. Unfortunately, for once in her life Miss Patterson didn't have a single useful bit of information. She sat on our front porch looking worried and somehow out of balance. If I'd been in a different frame of mind, I might have thought it was funny.

"Any luck?" Mrs. T. asked as we came inside.

Reluctantly I told her about the skiff we'd found. "We've got to go report it to Chief Partridge now. I don't think—"

"You two get in my car," she interrupted, grabbing up her pocketbook. "I'll take you up there. Let's not waste any time."

In a matter of minutes we were speeding toward Chief Partridge's office by the barbershop. Mrs. T.'s urgency scared me. Captain, always out of place on land, was absolutely terrified in the car. He sat on the back seat and gripped the armrest with a stubby hand.

May Cole, the dispatcher, was the only person in the chief's office. She smiled when she saw us, but her eyes were serious. The radio kept coming on with bits and pieces of information from first one and then another searcher.

"Captain and Neal have something for the Chief," Mrs. T. told her. "Where is he?"

"I'll locate him on the radio," May said. "Get ready, Neal, so you can tell him."

I cleared my throat and swallowed hard. After a minute or so May succeeded in finding the Chief and then thrust the microphone at me. My voice sounded trembly and thin.

"Captain Perry and I found Bill Blue's rowboat about a hundred yards out from shore, even with the Yardleys' place. It was drifting and had one oar. Someone had untied it—the rope wasn't broken. Captain says the boat stays at the landing and that . . . sometimes Georgie sits in it while it's tied up and pretends to row. We took it back to the landing and left it at the pier, if you want to look at it. That's all."

I turned away from the microphone.

"O.K., Neal, we'll check that out. Your folks are here with me." Chief Partridge spoke through the static. There was a click as he signed off. The tiny office seemed suddenly and ominously quiet.

"I don't think Georgie took that boat out," I said to the others. My voice got louder. "Looking for him on the river is just a waste of time! He was scared of the river, except when he was with Captain in the houseboat. He's hiding somewhere, scared out of his wits. And he'll be even more scared with all these people out looking for him. We ought to tell everyone to go home, then just Captain and I can look for him, and he'll come out from wherever he's hiding, and—"

A paper cup full of ice water appeared suddenly under my nose. May Cole stood over me with the water in one hand and a box of tissues in the other. I was crying again.

"They'll find him, Neal," she said. "Don't worry. The whole town is looking."

Captain and Mrs. T. tried to be reassuring, too. I stared past them across the room and out the window. Georgie, where are you? If we find you and you're O.K., then I promise . . . I promise . . .

"—to quit being phony," I said aloud between clenched teeth.

"What?" said Mrs. T

"Nothing," I answered. I blew my nose. "Come on. Let's go look some more."

By late afternoon the atmosphere of the search had become subdued. Folks had been sure Georgie would turn up quickly, but when he didn't and there was no clue, confidence turned to worry. Once again Mom, Dad, Aileen, and I met back at the house, this time in Dad's study with Chief Partridge.

"I hate to worry y'all," Chief drawled, "but if he don't turn up by tomorrow we got to think about two possibilities—the one that he started walking along the highway and got picked up by somebody, the other that he fell in the river. We got an all-points bulletin out in case of the first thing, but we might need to send down divers in case of the second."

Mom seemed to crumble inside when he said that. The four of us stared white-faced at each other, thinking the unthinkable. I still wanted to believe that Georgie hadn't been in the skiff, but until now no one else had come up with a satisfactory explanation for its being out in the river.

"Well," Dad said with a sigh, "I suppose you'd better do what you think is best."

The Chief went out and left us alone.

"I hope," said Mom, "we get another chance with Georgie."

Dad went over to the window. "With Georgie . . . with each other . . . all of us. It's a mess. I'm sorry."

Aileen caught my eye and raised one eyebrow. Her look seemed to telegraph, "Do tell!" but she said nothing. She is too much a cynic to expect overnight conversions.

I listened to his words, and I knew he meant them, that he was being as real and as honest as I'd ever known him to be. But too much had happened. If Georgie was dead, I didn't give a damn about Dad's remorse. It was too late. If we didn't find Georgie alive, I vowed I'd never spend another night under this roof, even if they sent me to reform school.

I got up abruptly. "I'm going out."

"You should eat something," Mom said, but I ignored her. I didn't know if I'd ever be able to eat again.

I threaded my way past the well-meaning people in the hall and on the front porch. They were acting like Georgie was already dead. All they lacked was tacking a white wreath on the damned door! I looked longingly across the street at Mrs. T.'s house, torn between the need to hide there and the need to find Georgie. Then with my hands in my pockets I headed toward Salton Street, keeping my eyes straight ahead to discourage people from stopping to talk. Maybe at the other end of town there was a quiet place up on the clay bluffs to sit and think.

I walked and walked. The slow, steady rhythm of my footsteps became a frame for some chords and a new tune fragment. When we found Georgie, I'd play it for him. I smiled inside, imagining the look on his face when he saw me play the piano. He'd be proud. I wished that I hadn't kept it from him. The melody played over and over in my head, and I began to improvise on it. I would call it "Georgie's Blues."

At the curb I waited as a couple of cars came along and turned the corner. It was here that Georgie had run away from me the morning we walked to school together.

The cars passed, and I crossed the street, trying to remember. Something important was lodged in my memory just out of reach. I couldn't quite grab it.

"Georgie's Blues" played on, and the little-boy image danced ahead of me faster and faster, then—

I stopped in my tracks, reliving that unreal moment when I'd been the victim of a magician's trick. Georgie had been there, and then he was gone. I'd never gotten a satisfactory explanation for it, from him or anyone else.

How did he do it? I began walking again, making a supreme effort to remember. He had fudged when I offered to walk with him to school. The missing reader wasn't missing at all. Then there was the can of soup and the candy bar in his book bag. They had to be part of the supplies he'd bought from Mr. Bailey. What a dummy I had been not to question him, but I was too wrapped up in my own problems that day even to think about Georgie.

My pace quickened. What if that day he'd planned to take the supplies to a hiding place he'd already picked out? And the only way he could do it was to get away from me so I wouldn't find the hiding place. It had to be somewhere nearby for him to be able to get there and still be in his schoolroom when I went looking for him.

Once again I found myself in front of the Tayntons' house with its flat yard and the border of irises. After a moment's hesitation I stepped over the flowers and into the yard. It didn't seem possible that Georgie could be anywhere around, but I went around to the back of the house just the same. A brindled cat came out from under the porch and flattened himself against the grass, watching me. Maybe Mrs. Taynton was peering at me through the window, wondering what I was doing sniffing around in her yard. There was a pecan tree, a small fenced-in garden plot, a sweet-bud bush. Nothing a person could hide in or behind. Beyond the yard was a vacant lot, and beyond that someone else's backyard.

The setting sun cast long shadows across the yard and the vacant lot, and maybe that's why I noticed the clump of vegetation in the far east corner. Kudzu and honeysuckle vine had completely covered something—it was hard to tell anything about the shape from where I stood.

The lot was full of weeds, but someone had trampled a narrow path through them, probably a shortcut to the next yard. I followed the path, but instead of going straight, it veered in the direction of the kudzu and honeysuckle. A few steps closer and I could see that the structure was an old abandoned chicken house—the kind with a tilted roof, completely enclosed on all sides except the one that faced east. Rusted chicken wire was nailed to the upper half of that side, but the whole thing was so covered with vines it was almost hidden from view.

For several minutes I stood in one spot, looking hard at the old chicken house and listening. It was a creepy place, where you'd expect to find spiders, rats, or snakes, not to mention poison ivy. I couldn't imagine Georgie having the courage to hide here, and yet—

Cautiously I picked my way through the tall grass. The door sagged on its hinges, held in place most likely by the stubborn vines. Looking down, I saw a fan-shaped mark in the weeds where the door had been opened and closed recently. The grass was bruised and trampled.

I took a deep breath, and, feeling like a complete fool, I whispered, "Georgie! It's me—Neal. Are you in there?"

Nothing. No sound.

"Georgie," I said, "there's nobody with me. Answer me, Georgie."

Still nothing.

I reached over and pulled open the rickety door.

CHAPTER 21

The doorway was only a little more than five feet high, so I had to bend over to look inside. Georgie would never in a million years hide in a shed like this. He's the original scaredy-cat when it comes to dark, creepy places. I had some trouble with it myself, half expecting a snake to slither over my feet.

The shed had a dirt floor swept clean, and it didn't smell too bad, considering it had been a chicken house. Whatever light there was came through the wire-covered side opening, the part that wasn't overgrown with vines. A rusty ax and some tobacco sticks stood in the far corner. Otherwise it was empty.

Or so I thought. I was about to back out and shut the door again, but something prompted me to step all the way inside for a final look.

That's when I saw him.

He was sitting Indian style in the back corner. The dim light on his pale skin made him seem even more pale—a tiny, silent ghost.

"Jesus!" I whispered. "God, Georgie, you scared shit out of me!"

He didn't move or speak. In the dimness I couldn't even tell whether or not he was looking at me. I went over and squatted in front of him.

"Georgie?"

His eyes behind the glasses stared flatly at me. They might have been the eyes of a turtle for all the recognition in them.

"It's me, Georgie—Neal. Are you O.K.?"

No response.

I reached out and touched his arm. The turtle eyes blinked once, but otherwise he was unmoving. The hairs rose on the back of my neck.

"Georgie, fella, I'm glad I found you! We . . . we were afraid you'd fallen in the river."

Silence. I felt like I was talking to a statue. What would get through to him? Was he playing games with me? I felt sick. He was too little for games, especially one like this.

"Captain's worried about you—he needs to see that you're safe."

No response.

I stood up to rest my cramped legs, wondering what to do. I saw then the little cache of supplies lined up along the wall beside him. Cans of soup, cans of milk, a box of crackers, a candy bar, and a bag of peanuts like the one he'd given me several days ago. So far as I could tell, though, nothing had been eaten

The silence stretched out. I heard my own breathing and the buzz of flies in the tangle of vines outside the shed. From a great distance I could make out the faint sputtering of boat motors on the river. Perhaps they were already planning where the divers would go down. I squatted again.

"Georgie, we've got to go back. Everyone's really worried. I'll stay with you. Nobody will do anything to you, I promise. Dad's sad about what he said to you. He won't—"

I stopped. All these words were meaningless to him. His stillness was ten times more frightening than if he'd been screaming and hysterical.

Should I leave him and go for help? I ruled out the option as soon as I thought of it. He might slip away while I was gone. Or if lots of people followed me back here, it might make matters worse. Somehow it seemed important to keep this place a secret. It was his—he had found it.

The shed was becoming noticeably darker. The only thing left to do was simply to pick him up bodily and take him home.

I opened the shed door as wide as it would go so I'd have plenty of room to get through the opening. Then I came back and bent over him.

"Georgie," I said softly, "it's time to go."

I slipped my left hand under his knees and grasped his body firmly in my right arm. He was strangely rigid, like someone under a spell. It was a struggle to hold onto him despite the fact he wasn't resisting. He was heavy. All the time I watched his face for signs of recognition or any kind of emotion, but nothing changed.

It was a relief to get outside the shed and straighten to my full height. I paused long enough to push the door shut with my heel, to keep it a secret for him.

The sun had gone down, but the western sky was full of gold light.

"See, Georgie?" I panted as I stumbled through the high weeds with my burden. "We're going to be back by bedtime. Mom and Dad and Aileen will be some kind of glad to see you. And Captain. You shouldn't have run away without telling Captain. It's been a hard day for him "

The stream of words came unchecked. I didn't even know why I was babbling on like that. Maybe to ward off evil spirits. Or maybe I thought if I kept talking something would penetrate that far-off place where his mind had gone.

I crossed the Tayntons' lawn and stepped over the iris border again, but this time because of Georgie I think I knocked down a couple of flowers. Mrs. Taynton called from her front porch swing.

"Heyo, Neal! Who you got there?"

"It's my little brother. He's . . . not doing so well."

She can move pretty fast for an old lady. "You come and sit down here on the step with him!" she ordered. "I'll go call your folks right this minute."

I didn't really want to stop, but my arms and back couldn't take much more, so I obeyed. I didn't want people to see him like this, but what could I do? I sank down on the steps and held him close to me.

"Hey, Georgie!" I whispered. "Come on, fella. It's going to be all right. You can come back now."

Shortly, Mrs. Taynton came out and eased down beside us on the steps. She smelled faintly of buttermilk. I steeled myself for some dumb remark, but she just studied Georgie's face without saying anything. Her wrinkled lips were pursed slightly, and she frowned. Finally she reached over and felt his forehead with one bony hand.

"No fever," she said, "but I expect a doctor needs to look at him all the same. Something's wrong."

Oh, boy, is it ever wrong! I thought, looking away from her. The throat ache came again, and my eyes filled up and spilled over. There wasn't a thing I could do about it either. The tears fell on Georgie, and my nose ran. Mrs. Taynton patted my arm and told me not to worry.

Then the peace was broken. Cars and people converged from half a dozen different directions. Chief Partridge roared up in his patrol car, bringing Mom and Dad with him. Mrs. T. had Captain in tow—I figured she must have fed him dinner. Pete and Aileen were together and Dad wasn't making anything of it. Others who had been searching seemed to rise out of the ground. News travels fast in Gideon. I had an insane urge to pick up Georgie and run, but it was out of the question. Instead I held him tight when Mom started to take him from my arms.

"I promised I'd stay with him," I said.

She peered closely at him, and her hand went to her mouth. "Oh, dear God, Richard! What's wrong with him?"

Dad was equally alarmed. They stared down at Georgie as though he were some extraterrestrial being.

Weird, I thought, feeling detached. What Georgie had been afraid of had happened. He had been replaced by this little person who looked like him, but who had no spirit inside.

'Where did you find him? What did he do when he saw you? What's the matter with him?" The questions buzzed around my head. I ignored them and held on to Georgie.

Mrs. T. moved closer. "We shouldn't waste any time getting him to a doctor. Call the Rescue Squad ambulance—it's down by the waterfront."

"Dr. Koch," Mom murmured. "Someone should tell Dr. Koch we're on our way."

It's hard to remember everything that happened afterward. Mostly I recall pieces of things, in no particular order. Not even the ambulance zooming up with its sirens screaming roused Georgie from his trance. Mom and I rode with him in the ambulance, Mrs. T. took Captain, and Dad and Aileen came along last in our car. I was glad Mrs. T. didn't leave Captain behind.

Since there's no hospital in Wayside, the doctor met us at his office. I stayed beside Georgie throughout the examination. His eyes were open all the time, and once in a while he'd blink, but he just didn't seem to see anything outside himself.

Dr. Koch asked me a few questions—where I'd found him, what he was doing, that sort of thing. He wanted to know if we knew why Georgie had run away. No one said anything at first. Mom looked at Dad as though for permission to speak. I was afraid if I started talking I'd never stop. And Dad . . . he looked about seventy years old. All his defenses were shot.

"He . . . thought we didn't love him," he said after a long pause, as though saying the words broke something inside him.

"Well," said Dr. Koch, "he's had some sort of profound emotional shock. Physically he seems all right, but something has happened to him psychically. I'm not trained to treat this sort of thing. I'd strongly recommend your taking him to Hatboro to the clinic, the sooner the better."

"I'm going with him," I said. "I promised I wouldn't leave him."

Dr. Koch put a hand on my shoulder. "That would be fine,

Neal, if Georgie were able to take in the fact that you were with him. But it's probably going to be some time before he's aware I think it might be better for you to go back home for now."

So then there was all the fuss of deciding what was to be done, with Dr. Koch telephoning and making arrangements. I just walked out and went back to the waiting room where Mrs. T. and Captain were sitting. Nothing seemed real. None of this was happening to us. I couldn't remember what day it was, or even how it had begun. I had been awake for so long I was pretty sure I'd forgotten how to sleep.

"They want me to go home," I said to Mrs. T. "Maybe you could take me."

"My pleasure." She smiled. "You and Captain, too. We've had a good visit today, in spite of the trouble."

"I wish Georgie was going back with us," I mumbled, slumping into the chair beside Captain. He didn't say anything, but he put a hand on my arm and squeezed it, and I knew he wished it too, maybe even more than I did, if that's possible.

It was nearly eleven o'clock by the time the three of us got back to Gideon. Mom, Dad, and Aileen had gone on to Hatboro with Georgie, and I had agreed to go home. It didn't take much to persuade me. I wanted to be by myself.

But when we pulled up in front of the house after returning Captain to his houseboat, the prospects of my being alone didn't look good at all. Cars were parked on both sides of the street, and every downstairs light was blazing.

"Maybe you'd better stay at my place tonight," Mrs. T. said, reading the look on my face.

"Nah—I'd rather be in my own bed. But how do I ask people in a polite way to get out?"

"I'll help." She got out and went inside with me.

I don't know how she managed, but in twenty minutes all those ladies and men were gathering up their stuff and leaving. She told them the news and assured them that everything was under control, and she said that I'd be fine by myself. She also told them I'd call them if I needed to, which was a lie, but if it would help them leave I wasn't going to argue.

So the house was finally cleared out.

Mrs. T. waited until the last car had driven away, and then she picked up her purse and sweater to leave, too.

"You're sure, now, you don't mind staying by yourself?"

I nodded. The way I felt, if I didn't see another person during the next twenty-four hours it would suit me fine.

"Well, if you change your mind, come on over. I'll put a blanket on the living room sofa for you and leave the side door unlocked."

The latch clicked shut behind her, and I took a deep, deep breath and exhaled. I went from room to room turning off lights. I ate some of the mounds of food that people had brought over. I locked the back door. The house seemed to become more and more quiet, like a balloon with the air leaking out slowly.

It was almost midnight and I started upstairs to bed because there was nothing left to do but sleep. The big mistake I made was to turn on the light in Georgie's room and look in.

And suddenly he seemed to be everywhere. I saw him at the table with his head bowed and his eyes squeezed shut. I saw him answering Mom's questions with infinite patience. Scampering up the plank to Captain's houseboat. Running ahead of me and disappearing. Holding onto my hand to anchor himself. Bowing under Dad's scathing words. Sitting Indian style in a chicken house, pale and unseeing. In an ambulance headed for a strange town.

I lowered myself onto his bed, feeling like someone had run into me headlong and knocked me breathless. As I sat there it seemed that the house was swelling inside, that rooms were expanding and somehow becoming emptier. I felt that if I stayed here I would vanish.

Without really thinking what I was doing or why, I ran to my room and pushed aside the clothes in the closet. There on the nail on its string was the church key I'd gone to so much trouble to get two years before. I snatched it and ran, down the stairs, out the front door. My feet pounded the sidewalk, and it seemed I was running faster than ever before in my life.

Maybe any other time I'd have been hesitant about going into the church at night, especially having to pass near the graveyard, but I never gave it a thought. I let myself in by the back way and went straight to the fuse box in the hall. I opened it and turned every single switch in it to ON. The church lit up like the morning sun. In the sanctuary I went from window to window, opening each one. The fresh night air poured into the stuffy atmosphere, sweetening and cooling. It was like opening a coffin.

Finally I sat down on the wobbly piano stool and opened the piano. The keys grinned comfortingly. I grinned back.

I began to play the melody I'd made in my head for Georgie—a blues. I played loud and clear.

"I'm not hiding any more!" I shouted to the walls. Music spilled and raced from my fingers.

"Are you surprised?" I yelled. "Aren't you amazed at old B-minus Sloan here? You didn't know he could play, did you? How d'ya like *this* kind of music? Whooooeeee—Lola Phifer's gonna di-ii-ii-ee of a-po-plex-eeeeee!"

The piano chuckled and yelled along with me. We made an awful lot of noise.

"I hid it from Georgie!" I screamed. "Even though he would have loved it so! I say, I hid it from my brother Georgie, even though he would've loved it so! This is *me*—Neal Sloan—the real Neal Sloan—and I ain't gonna hide no more!"

The piano and I—we stuffed that musty sanctuary so full of sound it couldn't hold it all. I improvised until my fingers felt bruised and the muscles in my back screamed at me to stop, for God's sake!

And finally I did.

And when I turned around on that squeaky, wobbly stool, I

saw dozens of people in the pews and in the aisles, some of them in bathrobes and pajamas. I saw Mr. Mac and Miss Patterson, Pete, Lola Phifer, and Mrs. T. among them. They were grinning and smiling and crying—and they stood up to clap. And when they started toward me, Mrs. T. was in the lead.